Clarkston Secrets

FRIENDSHIP AND SECRETS WE KEEP

JOHN RUSSELL

HOJOPRESS PUBLICATIONS

ISBN 979-8-9896331-6-6 (paperback)

ISBN 979-8-9896331-7-3 (ebook)

Book Cover by Sadia Asmir

For my daughter Samantha who fills my heart with joy each and
laughter every day
I love you.

Preface

In the heart of every town, amid its charming facade, lies a tapestry woven with threads of secrets, friendship, justice, and integrity. "Clarkston Secrets" is a story that takes you on a journey through the coastal town of Clarkston, where friendships are forged, secrets are unearthed, and the pursuit of justice and integrity is at the core of every action.

Friendship, the lifeblood of the community, binds the characters in this narrative. Their shared experiences, from joyful celebrations to daunting challenges, strengthen the ties that hold them together. Within this tight-knit group, they find solace, resilience, and unwavering support as they navigate the complexities in Clarkston.

Amidst the picturesque landscapes and gatherings, the pursuit of justice and integrity drives the story. The characters are drawn into an unexpected mission that uncovers the hidden underbelly of an organization dedicated to bettering the lives of the less fortunate. As secrets come to light, they embark on a quest to restore integrity and uphold justice for themselves and their community.

"Clarkston Secrets" explores the profound impact of friendship, the relentless pursuit of justice, and the unwavering commitment to integrity. Within these pages, you will find a story of resilience, growth, and the unbreakable bonds formed when individuals come together to confront the secrets that threaten the very heart of this beloved town.

Contents

Chapter 1

We stood together in front of our front yard, surveying the overgrown bushes and weeds that had taken over. I held a pair of gardening shears.

"It's time to tame this jungle!" I said with a mischievous grin.

Seth chuckled and responded, "You're right, Samantha!"

"We have our work cut out for us," I said, eyeing the overgrown bushes.

He laughed. "Remember last time? The thorns won."

"We'll win this round," I replied with a grin.

We worked in companionable silence for a while, the garden slowly transforming.

"You know," Seth said after a while. "This is kinda fun."

"Who knew gardening could be so rewarding?" I replied.

"Thanks for helping," he said.

"Anytime," I said. "It's nice spending time together."

Seth bent down, kissed me on the forehead, and smiled. "Agreed. We make a good team."

Our efforts inside the house persisted. He took the handyman role, armed with a toolbox and a can-do attitude, while I tackled the rooms with a paintbrush.

I couldn't resist teasing him. "Remember when you said you were 'handy?'"

He grinned and replied, "I might have exaggerated a bit, but I'm a quick learner!"

There were moments of hilarity when Seth attempted to assemble furniture. I witnessed with amusement as he juggled screws and instruction manuals, muttering to himself.

"Why do they make these things so complicated?" he grumbled. "It's just a bookshelf!"

I chuckled. "It's like a puzzle, dear. You love puzzles!"

Our home improvement escapades were not smooth sailing. Despite the chaos, they bonded with us and built cherished memories. We sat in our furnished living room, surrounded by the fruits of our labor. I experienced a profound sense of accomplishment.

The warm, golden embrace of the evening sun streaming through the bay window surrounded my new Clarkston home in a comforting glow. I had just given my closest friends a virtual tour of the house. Breanna, Holli, and Rebeccah were excited for me and about the upcoming wedding. I couldn't wait to see them.

Seth noticed a little stress I was holding. He came over to where I was standing.

"Samantha, what's weighing on you?"

I looked back at Seth. "You always know when something is bothering me. It is about my job. Mark has asked if I want to go into the field after my leave of absence. I let them know I would have a decision to make two weeks before I was due to return. We are coming up on two weeks, and I still don't know my answer. I am hoping our lives here in Clarkston will help me make a decision and help reassess my priorities."

"I still have the same stress that has brought me to the leave I have been taking." I took a substantial breath, allowing my voice to waver. Seth sat across from me. His eyes locked onto mine with concern.

"Seth," I began, "I need to reveal something to you, something I've kept locked away for a long time. It's about Operation Phoenix Rising." As I explained the mission, I recounted how it was a covert operation aimed at dismantling a drug cartel responsible for flooding our nation with narcotics. This mission marked my initiation into online forensics within the CIA.

Seth's eyes widened with each revelation as I spoke, reflecting his admiration for my skills and concern for the danger I encountered.

"My work with the CIA wasn't just a job. It was a life packed with secrets, dangers, and moral conflicts. I've seen and experienced things that have left an indelible mark on me."

I shared how the stress of living a double life and making split-second decisions had been a burden.

"Our move to Clarkston is more than just a fresh start. It's a lifeline. I want to focus on us for a while before deciding."

Seth's eyes softened with empathy, and his grip on my hand tightened. He spoke tenderly, "Samantha, I had no idea you went through all that. You've been through more than most can imagine, and it's no wonder you're seeking a quieter life now. You've more than earned it."

"Seth, I've never actually been in the field, and I'm quite happy with that."

Seth looked at me with a hint of surprise. "Really? I always thought you might be interested in the action out there."

I shook my head. "No, not at all. I'm content as a forensic specialist, working with computers and data analysis."

Seth raised an eyebrow. "It can be thrilling, the adrenaline rush."

"That's what I'm not after," I explained, meeting his gaze. "I find the controlled environment of the lab more appealing. The intricacies of forensics and decoding complex data fascinate me."

He considered this for a moment. "Don't you ever want to experience the thrill of the field?"

I paused, reflecting on his question. "Not really," I replied. "I've seen enough close calls and heart-pounding situations through the reports and evidence I analyze. I prefer to contribute to the team from behind the scenes. The adrenaline of the field may entice others, but I find my satisfaction in the quiet, methodical world of computer screens and data analysis."

"Let's wait to decide until after the wedding, and we have settled here," Seth added. "We need to do what's right for you."

I looked at him. "Thank you! I told Mark that I don't know if I would continue my work. Seated in the passenger seat of Seth's truck, I found solace in the engine's hum and my soon-to-be husband's comforting presence. We were on our way to Sunnyville, where our nuptials awaited us, and my heart was a tumultuous sea of feelings.

The anticipation of our marriage stirred a delightful blend of enthusiasm and happiness. The prospect of committing my life to Seth, my steadfast partner and confidant, infused my being with profound love and gratitude. I looked forward to beginning this new chapter alongside him. We would explore every nook and cranny of Clarkston's landscape.

The miles extended before us. I fixed my gaze upon the passing scenery beyond the window, grappling with the complex interplay of my past and present.

Chapter 2

The calm waves caressed the sandy shore, and the salty gust promised new beginnings. Pink and orange sky hues seemed to bless our love. Our ceremony was a beachfront affair in picturesque Sunnyville. Breanna, ever the daring and resourceful soul, had been through her union with Aaron two years ago and took charge of planning the entire beachside ceremony.

The sun descended below the horizon, and it embraced the sandy shore. My eyes gleamed with happiness and enthusiasm, mirroring the love that grew within my heart.

I wore a stunning, flowy bridal gown that flowed with the overdraft. The bodice was embellished with delicate lace, and the skirt cascaded to the ground, enhanced with intricate embroidery. My smile shone with love and happiness. I held a bouquet of wildflowers, and my blonde hair blew in the wind. The gentle colors of the flowers complemented the natural surroundings, adding a hint of whimsy to the elegance of the occasion.

Breanna gasped, "Oh my gosh, Samantha, you look stunning! That gown is perfect for you!"

Rebeccah, the sentimental and poetic soul, smiled and added, "Seth is going to be speechless."

Their words of admiration and love only added to my nervousness. It was heartwarming to know that my friends saw the splendor and significance of the gown. Their compliments made me feel even more confident and glowing on my wedding day. Their company was invaluable, and I realized their genuine joy for Seth and me would make it all the more memorable.

Holli touched my shoulder with her serene and poised demeanor. "Samantha," she said, "we've got everything under control. Why don't you take a few moments for yourself? Breathe and relax. We'll be right outside when you're ready."

Rebeccah stated, "Yes, let this sink in. Your journey has been incredible, and you deserve it."

With a smile, Breanna said, "Take a step back from the whirlwind, and when you're ready, we'll be here to celebrate with you."

I gazed at my reflection in the mirror and marveled at the transformation. The woman who had once been a professional and concealed her identity under layers of classified information was now a glowing bride.

The scent of wildflowers from my bouquet filled the room. I couldn't help but smile. The gust coming through the open window carried the salty smell of the sea. I closed my eyes, letting the breeze play with my hair, and sensed liberation. My heart filled with gratitude as I took a deep breath.

The wedding celebration was about to start. Breanna, Holli, and Rebeccah stood beside me, beaming in their dresses. Each bridesmaid's gown mirrored their style and personality, yet they created a harmonious and beautiful picture when they stood together.

Their encouragement and friendship meant the world to me. Their unwavering help throughout the nuptial planning process had been a lifeline.

Walking down the aisle toward Seth, I stole glances at him. My heart fluttered with happiness. His stare fixed on me as if I were the most beautiful and captivating sight he had ever seen. His smile reached his eyes, and they sparkled with tenderness.

Happiness showed in his eyes, a reminder that, like me, he embarked on a new chapter in our lives. The world faded, leaving only our unbreakable bond. Reaching him at the altar, his hand extended.

Seth's eyes never left mine. He listened to our vows, and his eyes softened with emotion as we exchanged promises of love and dedication. I viewed a future filled with love and laughter. A stare said he would encourage me in good times and bad and that we might conquer anything that came our way together.

We said our "I dos" and sealed our love with a kiss. The wedding reception occurred in a picturesque beachside venue enhanced. Fairy lights, lanterns, and floral decorations created a dreamy and enchanting atmosphere. The waves crashing against the shore provided a soothing backdrop as the sun descended, casting a golden glow over the festivities.

Guests mingled and chatted. The dance floor was energetic as friends and family twirled and swayed to the music. The DJ played a mix of romantic ballads and upbeat songs, catering to everyone and ensuring that the floor remained packed.

Long tables arranged with elegant white tablecloths and centerpieces of fresh flowers added a hint of sophistication to the venue. The aroma of delicious food floated through the air, enticing everyone to indulge in the gourmet dishes and desserts.

Glowing, Breanna stood at the center of attention, holding a microphone with a smile illuminating her face. Her red auburn hair cascaded over her shoulders, framing her expressive eyes. The clinking of glasses and the murmur of hushed conversations fell silent as she spoke. The guests turned their attention toward her. She began her speech with a sincere and heartwarming tone.

"Good evening, everyone," Her voice filled with affection. Today, we are here to celebrate Samantha and Seth's union and share in the happiness of their adventure together. I am honored to stand here as Samantha's matron of honor and speak on behalf of all her friends and loved ones."

"We celebrate Samantha and Seth's love today," her eyes glimmered with emotion, "I'm reminded of the saying that friendship is like a fine wine; it gets better with time. Samantha and I have been friends for so long. We have had an incredible journey, from beach umbrella battles to culinary escapades."

The guests chuckled.

"My dear friends," Breanna continued, "what matters is not the mishaps or the misadventures but the connection that has seen us through it all. Samantha, you've always been the kind of friend who brings laughter, kindness, and love into our lives. You've found a love that complements your spirit. We all knew something was between you two when you met Seth in Kodiak. I stand here today, looking at the love and bliss in your eyes. I can say that you've found your soulmate."

She looked at Seth and I, our eyes locked in an affectionate embrace.

"To Samantha and Seth," Breanna raised her glass higher, "may your adventure overflow with joy and unforgettable moments like our friendship. Here's to a love that grows stronger with time, just like a fine wine."

Breanna's toast was complete when I caught a glimpse of something out of the corner of my eye, giving me the unsettling feeling of being watched. This instinctive reaction was one I didn't like, but I tried to downplay it, convincing myself that my mind was just playing tricks on me.

The wedding reception continued, and Seth's family took the microphone and offered their toast to the newlyweds. The atmosphere in the room shifted, reflecting the unique dynamics and personalities within Seth's family.

First up was his dignified and reserved father, who had always taken his responsibilities seriously. He stood with pride. His eyes swelled with affection as he looked at Seth and Samantha. His toast was filled with wisdom and fatherly advice, emphasizing the importance of love, respect, and communication in a marriage. He wanted the best for his son and new daughter-in-law, and his words conveyed a sense of sincerity and genuine blessing.

After Seth's father's address, his younger sister took the floor. Her toast - full of energy and enthusiasm - brimmed with childhood anecdotes, prompting humor and fond recollections from the guests. A profound undercurrent of love and encouragement emerged amid tales of sibling rivalry. Her remarks and comments brought a youthful joy and energy to the room.

His best friend, who was a brother, gave a toast with humor and sentiment. He recounted stories of their adventures and escapades, reminding everyone of the deep bond of a relationship that had been a constant in his life. His remarks injected a hint of lightheartedness into the proceedings and celebrated the importance of lifelong friends in one's journey.

Our first dance was emotional and beautiful. Seth and I stepped onto the floor. All eyes were on us. The venue had twinkling fairy lights and delicate lanterns that cast a romantic radiance over everything. The floor was a work of art decorated with intricate floral designs that contributed to the enchanting atmosphere.

In my flowing gown, I felt like a princess. I gazed into Seth's eyes and saw his love for me, which comforted me. And I knew this moment would linger in our memories. The melody of our chosen first dance filled the air, its lyrics echoing commitment and shared dreams. Thus, we swayed and danced to the music.

Halfway through the song, the DJ announced, inviting other couples to join us on the dance floor. The tradition signaled the beginning of a celebration involving everyone. Couples of all ages and backgrounds joined us on the floor, creating a beautiful tableau of togetherness. There were young couples, their eyes shining with the promise of a future together. Older couples also weathered life's difficulties, holding each other close and swaying to the music.

Chuckles echoed throughout the room, and the rustling of elegant dresses and sharp suits was heartwarming. The swishing of feet gliding on the dance floor represented the enduring power of love and the joy of celebrating it with our friends and family.

Seth and I continued to dance, surrounded by the people we loved the most, our smiles never fading. The music swelled, and as the song reached its crescendo, we exchanged grateful glances. The dance ended, and everyone erupted in applause and cheers. It had been a magical moment, one that we would treasure forever.

The evening unfolded, and the atmosphere grew even more festive. It was due to delightful surprises and activities that our thoughtful friends, Holli and Rebeccah, arranged. These surprising elements incorporated an extra layer of celebration into our reception.

First was the charming photo booth, an oasis of creativity. Its colorful props and whimsical backdrops beckoned to our guests, encouraging everyone to step inside and create memories. People donned silly hats, oversized sunglasses, feather boas, and other playful accessories, filling the room with joyous laughter.

Holli, who always had an infectious enthusiasm, couldn't help but be the first to dive into the photo kiosk, dragging Rebeccah along with her. Their giggles and playful antics determined the tone for what was to come. Holli asked us to join the fun as they posed for the camera. With each snapshot, the room overflowed with the sounds of carefree giggles and the click of the camera, capturing cherished moments.

As the night progressed, we discovered another surprise our creative friends orchestrated. This time, it was a video booth where our loved ones could express their genuine wishes and messages for us. Holli took charge enthusiastically, encouraging guests to approach the camera and share their thoughts.

The questions she raised were thought-provoking and heartwarming, leading to touching responses. Guests offered us advice, their fondest memories of us as a couple, and their hopes for our future together. The video booth became a place of genuine emotion and heartwarming expressions of love.

It was time for one of the most cherished traditions—cutting the cake. Seth and I made our way to the elegant table. It was a masterpiece, a stunning three-tiered creation decorated with intricate designs mirroring the sand patterns beneath our feet. The fairy lights and flicker of candles made the moment even more magical.

Seth and I shared a conspiratorial smile as we stood side by side. Our hands met on the knife's handle, and we made the first incision into the cake's delicate layers. The sound of camera shutters clicking captured the moment for posterity. With a laugh, Seth and I shared bites of the delicious confection. The cake was a treat.

The night reached its dazzling climax as the sky above erupted in a spectacular fireworks display. My heart surged with emotions as the vibrant colors painted the night sky, casting a mesmerizing backdrop for Seth's and my grand exit.

The gasps and cheers from our friends and family mingled with the crackling sounds above. We bid farewell to our friends, embarking on their adventures. I stood there, and my heart increased with overwhelming emotions.

I caught a fleeting glimpse of my boss, Mark Vento. He was after my answer if I wanted to go into the field. Why would he be at my wedding? He knew I wasn't prepared to give him an answer. His abrupt appearance and vanishing act left me feeling like he had never been there.

Seth detected the change in my demeanor and asked, "Is everything okay?"

I hesitated, torn between addressing the issue and not wanting to disrupt our day. I replied with a forced smile, "It's nothing, just a surprise I didn't expect."

With Seth by my side, I sensed I could conquer anything ahead. Our love was a commitment to stand together through all the tomorrows that awaited us. I was filled with hope, excitement, and gratitude. Today marked the beginning of a new chapter.

Chapter 3

Settling into our new life in Clarkston, after the joyous beachside wedding in Sunnyville, brought a breath of fresh air. Clarkston seemed plucked straight from the pages of a storybook. Among Clarkston's highlights, its breathtaking natural beauty stood out.

The town was surrounded by rolling hills, expansive forests, and sparkling lakes, making it a haven for outdoor enthusiasts. The nearby hiking trails offer opportunities for scenic walks and invigorating adventures. The lakes provided a serene setting for kayaking, fishing, or simply enjoying the peacefulness of nature.

News traveled through the grapevine. It revealed that the town cared for one another. In times of need, they extended a helping hand, and in moments of joy, the city celebrated together. They always wanted to help people. The quaint village welcomed us with open arms.

Whispers in town about the upcoming artisan craft fair at the civic center created an irresistible buzz of eagerness. This exhibition was just one of many events uniting the people of Clarkston. Attending was spontaneous, serving as the perfect way to immerse ourselves. We anticipated exploring unique artworks, intricate jewelry, and crafted goods.

The melodies of acoustic guitars and the faint laughter of families greeted us as we arrived at the civic center. The crisp autumn air carried the scent of baked pastries and coffee. The fair's atmosphere was alive with the chatter of friends catching up and children's excited exclamations as they admired the artisanal wonders on display.

Seth and I strolled hand in hand through the bustling artisan craft fair. I was drawn to one booth - lively and creative.

We had the pleasure of encountering Rachel. She was a seasoned artisan whose skill and commitment were etched into the lines of her weathered yet gentle hands. Her booth was a veritable wonderland of handwoven scarves, shawls, and blankets, each masterpiece of intricate patterns.

"Seth, look at this," I exclaimed, my eyes lit up with excitement. "These scarves are stunning. The colors and patterns are so vibrant and unique. It's like you've captured the essence of Clarkston's natural beauty in your work."

With a warm smile behind her display, Rachel replied, "Thank you so much. I draw a lot of inspiration from this wonderful town and its surroundings. It's a special place."

Seth said, "I'm fascinated by your work. How long have you been an artisan here in Clarkston?"

Rachel's eyes sparkled as she reminisced, "I've been part of this community for about five years, and it's been an incredible journey. The people here are so supportive, and the natural beauty is a constant source of inspiration."

"We're fairly new to Clarkston." I shared, "We moved here recently. But we've been amazed by the warmth and creativity of this town."

Seth nodded, and added, "Absolutely. We're looking forward to getting more involved in the community. Any events or groups you recommend for newcomers like us?"

Rachel's face lit up with enthusiasm, "Welcome to Clarkston! There are plenty of opportunities to get involved. There's a town meeting coming up next week. It's a great way to meet more folks and learn about what's happening here."

We purchased one of Rachel's handwoven scarves, and bid our farewell.

We strolled away, the charming streets of Clarkston came alive with the sights and sounds. Laughter echoed from nearby cafes, and the windows of boutique shops displayed handcrafted items.

I pointed out one of the posters. "Look, Seth," I said, "a gala for a charity called 'Hope for Tomorrow' is coming soon. The purpose is to help the children of Clarkston have a better tomorrow. It's a cause I can be passionate about."

Seth nodded, "That sounds like a fantastic time. Let's go."

Later that afternoon, I began my research journey, firmly establishing roots in the town I had grown to love. My heart swelled with the desire to make a meaningful impact on my new home. I was intrigued by the Hope for Tomorrow charity and eagerly wanted to learn more about it and how I could contribute. My exploration led me to their website, and I found that the charity's purpose aligned with my values. Every word I read about the positive transformations in "Hope for Tomorrow" plunged me into action. I was determined to contribute, so I set my sights on a vacated position on the Board of Directors. My skills and boundless passion could breathe life into their movement.

I needed to earn some money while on my leave of absence. I found the 'Hope for Tomorrow' board member application online and began to complete it. I stopped to ponder the field that asked for my "current job," and a wistful smile touched my lips. I couldn't list my exhilarating role as a "computer genius for the CIA" as much as it would have been impressive. I reflected on a different yet rewarding chapter of my life—my college experience of lending a helping hand at a summer camp. The memories of that time brought warmth to my heart.

Later that afternoon, I was ecstatic to receive an invitation for an initial screening interview, igniting a surge of anticipation and excitement. The appointed time arrived. I climbed into my SUV and headed towards Hope for Tomorrow's home offices nestled in the heart of downtown Clarkston.

Upon stepping into the HR department's office, a serene ambiance surrounded me, bathed in a tranquil light that eased my nerves. The welcoming smile from the friendly receptionist immediately calmed any lingering jitters I had. My heart raced. The clock ticking reminded me of the significant opportunity ahead.

But my nervous energy melted away once I was in, and everything was fine. During my interview with the HR manager, I discussed my qualifications and aspirations for the position, highlighting my passion for community involvement and youth empowerment. I shared past experiences, such as leading mentorship programs for at-risk youth and coordinating a community garden initiative, which showcased my commitment and hands-on approach. We explored how my values align with "Hope for Tomorrow" and my vision for expanding outreach programs to support young people's development.

The HR manager expressed a genuine interest in my experiences and how they would help me contribute to the organization. We delved into my past projects, where I emphasized the importance of mentorship and community engagement. Our dynamic conversation renewed my enthusiasm for the role, and I left the interview feeling optimistic and excited about the possibility of making a difference with "Hope for Tomorrow."

I gathered my things to begin to leave. "Thank you. I'm excited about possibly working together and making a difference."

"We'll be in touch soon to schedule the next steps," she said, extending her hand with a warm smile.

I shook her hand, grateful for the opportunity. "I look forward to it," I said. "Thank you for your time."

I returned home after the intense interview, my heart still racing. Seth was waiting for me with a glass of wine and a comforting sight after the eventful night.

"How did it go?" We settled into the cozy living room.

Taking a sip of wine, I found the experience intense yet refreshing. The members asked probing questions to understand my qualifications and potential organizational contributions. Seth, curious, asked how I responded, and I explained how I conveyed my commitment to the cause and outlined a clear vision for the organization, leaving me with a sense of optimism.

Seth raised his glass, clinking it against mine. "You did well. Your passion must have shone."

My phone buzzed, and I picked it up. It was an email notification, and the subject line read, "Board of Directors Application Status." With trembling hands, I clicked to open it. The email was from Dakota Tampani. His name alone sent hope through me.

The message began with warm thanks for my loyalty and enthusiasm for the charity. I read on, my heart skipped a beat, and it soon became apparent that this was not just a polite rejection email. Mr. Tampani expressed the board's unanimous decision to invite me to join the Board of Directors.

Tears of joy welled up in my eyes as I continued to read. The board members were impressed with my commitment, ideas, and dedication to empowering underprivileged youth in Clarkston. They believed I would be a valuable addition to the team and invited me to become a board member.

I couldn't contain myself as I read those words. This opportunity was a moment of pure delight and validation. Those in attendance had seen in me my potential, and I was honored. I knew I had discovered my true calling in this charming town.

The night of my first board meeting was finally here, and I was excitedly buzzing. "I can't believe it's finally happening," I exclaimed, my voice filled with excitement.

Seth grinned in response, his eyes reflecting my enthusiasm. "You've worked so hard for this moment," he remarked, his words imbued with pride. "I know you'll do great," he added.

I drove over to the Hope for Tomorrow offices and parked my car. Once inside, I met other board members and got to know their names and what committees they were a part of. They came from many diverse backgrounds, and I shared my IT experience.

Bobby Guzman approached me, "Do you know any good accounting software programs? I used to work at Bells and Stuff, but we were not automated and certainly not on the Cloud."

"I do know of some that are good and secure from both cyber and physical threats," I added.

Intrigued, Bobby asked, "Can we install it on our network?"

"I am sure that can be arranged," I said, willing to help however I could.

Dakota introduced me. The charity saw significant growth and success, but it had some economic downfalls over the past years. Dakota was brought in to help with the growth. The non-profit garnered positive attention and donor support, further solidifying Tampani's reputation as an effective and dedicated leader.

Dakota led the meeting professionally. The discussion turned to program updates, and Dakota provided insights into their initiatives. Stephanie, who oversaw youth outreach, shared heartwarming success stories about young lives impacted by our programs.

"Stephanie, your work with the youth has been remarkable," said Dakota.

The meeting flowed seamlessly, touching on topics like expanding youth outreach, engaging more volunteers, and reviewing the organization's financial reports. We scrutinized the figures, ensuring transparency and accountability in our operations.

Our Dedicated Initiatives Director, Erin Flanigan, prepared the floor to present a report on the year's achievements. With passion and eloquence, Erin began to narrate the organization's notable accomplishments.

"Ladies and gentlemen of the board," Erin addressed us, "I'm thrilled about our achievements over the past year."

She painted a vivid picture of the growth in our mentorship programs, her voice carrying the weight of its positive impact on young individuals. The connection between students and their experienced mentors was highlighted as a source of invaluable guidance and unwavering support, a tribute to our organization's dedication to nurturing the potential of the youth we served.

Erin moved on to our fundraising achievements. Her eyes gleamed with pride and gratitude. The overwhelming generosity experienced not only met but exceeded our expectations. It was more than just financial support; it was a resounding vote of confidence in our mission. The room swelled with a shared sense of accomplishment, reinforcing our ability to make a meaningful difference.

Fundraising strategies were on the agenda, a topic close to my heart. "The gala is a fantastic opportunity to raise vital funds and spread awareness," I said.

As the report drew close, Erin's voice resonated with a profound sense of fulfillment. She shared stories of young individuals whose lives had been transformed through our programs. The stories were inspiring, proving the power of education, mentorship, and community support. It left everyone in the room dedicated to our cause.

Ally emphasized the need to allocate funds effectively to benefit youth programs. I agreed, stressing that efficient fund distribution is essential for maximizing our impact on the community's young people.

Dakota's closing remarks resonated with me. "Let's remember why we're here," he said.

Dakota approached me with a smile as I gathered my notes and prepared to leave the conference room.

"Samantha," Mr. Tampani began, his tone filled with appreciation, "I wanted to thank you for your contributions. Your ideas for the gala are inspiring."

I blushed slightly at the compliment. "Thank you, Mr. Tampani. I believe this event can raise a significant amount of money."

Dakota nodded in agreement. "Samantha. I share your zeal, and I do not doubt that your leadership will make this function a remarkable success. Remember, don't hesitate to reach out if you need additional assistance or resources. We're all in this together."

I appreciated the encouragement. "Thank you for your kind words. I'm excited about the possibilities and committed to making the event a night to remember."

I grabbed my purse and went out the door, but I heard a loud discussion. It was a heated conversation between two prominent figures within our organization.

I approached, and the clash of voices grasped my attention. It was Emily Raymond, our financial expert, her brows furrowed in concentration and her words certain. Opposite her stood Bobby Guzman, a seasoned board member persistent in attention to detail. I kept myself from their eyes as I had mine on them.

I felt foreboding as I wondered how this clash would turn out. Their voices were tense, and it was evident that they were engaged in an intense argument. I got closer and eavesdropped on their conversation.

"We need to address these discrepancies immediately," Emily said, her tone firm. "Transparency and accuracy in our financial reporting are critical. If we ignore these issues, we could face significant economic problems within Hope for Tomorrow."

Bobby responded, "Emily, I think you're blowing this out of proportion," his frustration evident. "Our financial practices have always been sound, and the data presented here is no different. There's no need to alarm everyone with unfounded concerns."

Emily's eyes narrowed, and she leaned forward. "Bobby, these are not unfounded concerns. The discrepancies are right here in black and white. We owe it to our donors and the people we serve to ensure everything is above board."

Bobby's face reddened as he crossed his arms. "I'm telling you, Emily, there's nothing to worry about. We've always managed our finances with integrity. Just because there are a few anomalies doesn't mean there's a systemic problem."

Their disagreement revolved around the interpretation and handling of financial data, and it was clear that both were deeply upset. I listened to their exchange, and wondered if these discrepancies were isolated incidents or indicative of more significant economic issues lurking beneath the surface. I needed to gather more information and assess the situation before acting.

Sitting at my desk, I opened my laptop and began accessing Hope for Tomorrow's digital records.

I spent a lot of time reviewing the financial statements and comparing the numbers, looking for any discrepancies Emily had mentioned during her argument with Bobby. It was a tedious process that involved working with spreadsheets full of numbers that showed how the organization was doing economically.

I combed through the fiscal statements, cross-referenced the numbers, and looked for any inconsistencies Emily had mentioned during her argument with Bobby. It was a painstaking process that involved navigating through spreadsheets populated with rows and columns of numbers that represented the organization's economic health.

I scrutinized balance sheets and traced transactions back and forth. I had to analyze each entry, every debit, credit, and note. It was like solving a jigsaw puzzle, where the pieces were fiscal data points. The picture formed held the key to understanding the organization's economic situation.

In simple terms, this digital treasure hunt carried severe consequences. The path to unraveling this budgetary mystery twisted and turned. I was committed to following it wherever it led, exposing uncomfortable truths that emerged as a necessary risk.

I needed to safeguard the charity's integrity. The minutes turned into hours, and I became one with the data, inching closer to the answers hidden in the numbers.

The incident in the corridor encouraged me to dig into these economic discrepancies and ensure the organization's integrity.

Everything appeared to be in fiscal order, but over several monthly meetings, I spotted minor discrepancies in the financial statements presented during our board meetings. The numbers didn't quite match the expenses recorded. There needed to be funds, unexplained payments, and duplicate transactions. I couldn't ignore the gnawing sensation in my gut that something was wrong.

Sitting in my cozy home office with a lone potted plant on the window, I confided in my closest friends, Breanna, Holli, and Rebeccah. We may have moved to different cities thanks to technology, but our friendship remained as strong as ever.

I opened a Zoom call, and soon, their familiar faces filled my screen. "Hey, guys," I greeted them with a smile, trying to hide the concern that lingered beneath the surface.

"Hey, Sam! How's life in Clarkston treating you? What is wrong with the plant behind you?" Breanna asked, with that signature wisdom that she liked to flaunt.

I grin at her. "Well, Bre, the plant is fine. It just needs a little TLC, and I can't give it to them right now because I am busy programming another toaster. I'm also not handing out sage advice like you, but I'm getting there. Seriously, I've started working for an organization called Hope for Tomorrow. It's like trying to herd cats, but I feel I'm exactly where I need to be."

"That's amazing! We knew you'd make a difference," Holli said, her words laced with encouragement.

Rebeccah added humor to the mix, saying, "And don't forget to send us postcards from you when you're a big-shot board member!"

Our laughter echoed through the virtual space, reminding me.

I wanted to focus on the positives, but I couldn't shake the troubling thoughts about the organization's finances. I took a deep breath and shared my concerns with my friends. "Something is bothering me."

"What is it?" Rebeccah asked, her eyes filled with concern.

I delved deeper into the records, and some irregularities raised red flags. Unexplained expenses, discrepancies in revenue sources, and a pattern of unusual payments to specific vendors warranted further investigation. I knew that sometimes the devil was in the details, and I was determined to uncover hidden truths buried in the digital records."

"Do we need to come out and see you?" Breanna asked.

Rebeccah chimed in, "And we make quite a formidable team."

"It's settled," Holli declared. "We'll be there by tomorrow, right, ladies?"

"Yes!" both Rebeccah and Breanna exclaimed in unison.

I couldn't resist a bit of playful banter with my friends. "Oh, I see how it is, teaming up on me as usual, huh?"

Breanna chuckled, "Well, you know we've got to keep you guessing."

Rebeccah said, "That's right, a little friendly team rivalry."

With her characteristic humor, Holli added, "Besides, you can handle all three of us, can't you?"

Samantha laughed, grateful for their support, and shared a sense of humor. "Ladies, I can't wait to see you tomorrow!"

"So, what is our initial plan?" asked Rebeccah.

"It's essential not to make conclusions without evidence," Holli advised. "It should be approached with caution."

Breanna nodded, "Maybe we can gather some information to corroborate your suspicions."

"A good plan," Rebeccah agreed, always ready for a challenge.

"I have a thought. There's a Gala scheduled in Clarkston during your stay, and I'd love for all of you to attend as my guests," I expressed with a smile. "It would mean a lot to me, and I'm sure you'll enjoy the experience."

Their faces lit up with excitement at the prospect. Breanna, always one to appreciate a good event, exclaimed, "A Gala? Count me in! I've been itching to get all dressed up for something like that!"

Holli chimed in, "It's a fantastic idea, Samantha. We can combine business and pleasure by attending the Gala while we're there."

Rebeccah added, "I'm all for it! I'll even help you find the perfect outfit, Samantha."

"Hey, guys," I greeted them with a smile, trying to hide the concern that lingered beneath the surface. "So, about the Gala, it's not just a fancy party. It's a significant fundraiser for Hope for Tomorrow, the organization I'm involved with. This year, the Gala aims to raise funds for our new Hope Haven project. It's a transitional housing program for homeless families, providing them with a safe space and resources to get back on their feet.

I looked at all of them on the screen. "The Gala is vital for us because it's not only a funding source. It is a platform to raise awareness about the homelessness crisis in Clarkston."

Breanna's expression was thoughtful as she absorbed the information. She nodded and said, "I'm glad we can participate in the event."

Holli, with a determined look, stated, "This Gala just got a lot more meaningful."

"Yes, it did," I continued. "Who else would I want to spend it than on my three most favorite people in the world."

We said our goodbyes and the Zoom call ended.

I was excited about the Zoom call and finally seeing the ladies. However, something was still gnawing at me. I went to Seth and leaned over. "I need to talk to you about something."

He looked at me with concern and held my hand. "What is it?"

"We need to discuss the financial discrepancies I found in the records,"

"What did you find?" His expression turned concerned.

"Several irregularities in the accounts," I replied, detailing the findings.

"This is concerning," his brow furrowing.

Looking at him, "It's crucial we address these issues promptly,".

"I agree. We can't afford to overlook potential problems," he nodded thoughtfully. I'm glad you shared this with me, Sam," It's essential
to address these concerns."

His words strengthened me, and I felt reassured knowing he was by
my side.

"We need more evidence before making accusations," I stated firmly.

"I'm here to help in any way I can during the investigation.".

I was determined to uncover the matter.

Chapter 4

The doorbell chimed. Its cheerful tone cut through the air like a triumphant note in a harmonious composition.

Breanna's voice, laden with teasing, "Sam, are you ready for the invasion of the troublemakers?"

Holli smiled, "Trust you've stocked up on snacks. We've got appetites as big as our brains."

Rebeccah winked, "And don't forget, we're here to solve mysteries, so keep them coming!"

Their banter was a sweet reminder of the joy that defined our friendship. I welcomed them with open arms, knowing this reunion would be saturated with laughter and playful mischief.

"Welcome to Clarkston!" I exclaimed, my eyes lighting up as I witnessed the amazement in their faces. "Seth sends his love. He is away on business catching the bad guys." I exclaimed with genuine joy. "Thank you for coming. I've missed you so much!"

Breanna gave me a playful grin. "We wouldn't miss it for the world, Sam! You understand we're always here for you."

Holli nodded. "We're in this together. You can count on us. Let's begin to work!"

"Thank you all," I said. "I can't express how much it means to have you here. It's a captivating little town, and I'm sure you'll love it as much as I do."

My friends were enchanted by the scenery and the quaint downtown area. The small shops and boutiques lining the roads captivated them, and I could tell they were enjoying the atmosphere. With its vibrant, tree-lined streets and historic architecture, Clarkston appealed to me. The tight-knit town thrived on neighborly interactions. It was a place where people cared for one another. The heartwarming smiles and greetings exchanged between neighbors were evidence of the community's warmth.

We strolled through Clarkston, and I saw my friends take in the lure and beauty. The small shops and boutiques lining the roads captivated them.

"Oh, this place is adorable, something out of a storybook!" Breanna exclaimed, her eyes darting from one boutique to another. "I could spend hours exploring all these shops."

Holli nodded. "It's so lovely and peaceful here. I can understand why you fell in love with this town. Everyone is so friendly and welcoming," she remarked, smiling at a couple of locals passing by.

We took a break at a coffee shop, where brewed coffee's rich, earthy scent called us. We placed our orders, and the barista, whose nametag stated her name was Makenzie, glanced at me and smiled.

Makenzie's eyes sparked curiosity as she extended a friendly welcome, "It's a pleasure to meet all of you."

"See, that is the celebration I told you about, and we are going," I proudly said, pointing to the poster.

Makenzie's warm smile held a tinge of nostalgia as she leaned. Her voice softened, and she said, "Hope for Tomorrow played a huge role in my family when I was a child. They provided us with food and paid for my summer camp every year. It meant the world to us."

Her words painted a vivid picture of the past, and her eyes shimmered with emotion, "But this year, it's a bit different. I discovered that there are not enough funds to continue that program and their after-school care. It's disheartening to know how much it impacted my life in such a positive way."

A deep sense of empathy washed over me as I listened to Makenzie's poignant story. Her words underscored the charity's positive impact and the pressing need to regain its ability to continue helping those in the neighborhood.

Our encounter at the coffee shop with Makenzie brought the pressing issues at Hope for Tomorrow into sharp focus. Hearing about the support Makenzie's family in the past, ensuring she might attend summer camp, was heartwarming. The revelation that there are not funds to provide these vital services was troubling.

I looked at the women. "I knew funds were low, but I did not know how it would impact people."

A contemplative calm settled over our group as we processed the emotional weight of Makenzie's story. Breanna, ever willing to delve into the emotional depths of a situation, broke the silence. Her voice, soft but unwavering, "We need to set this right for all those who rely on these services."

Nods rippled through our group, a collective determination taking hold. We were friends gathered for a reunion and champions of justice. Together, we were committed to uncovering the truth and restoring the organization's integrity that held so much meaning for the town.

We exited the coffee shop, and the golden sunlight bathed Clarkston's charming streets, giving the town an even more inviting ambiance. Our group proceeded to chat and soak in the surroundings. It wasn't long before we encountered a group of friendly locals gathered in a small park nearby.

We found my vehicle and got inside to go back to my house. It was quiet. I contemplated the charity's impact on the community.

Breanna turned to us and said, "Her story touched my heart. It's evidence of your incredible work for this town."

"Did you realize,' I began, "that Clarkston has an annual 'Pie in the Face' charity event? People volunteer to have pies thrown at them, and the proceeds go to local charities. It's both hilarious and heartwarming!"

Holli raised an intrigued eyebrow. 'Pie in the Face, huh? I'm in. I've always wanted to see if I can dodge a pie.'

Rebeccah chuckled with a mischievous glint in her eye and included, 'Count me in too, but only if I can throw the pie.'

Our laughter echoed the car as we discussed the Pie in the Face event and our plans for it.

We arrived at my house and went inside. Sinking into the plush couches, relaxation washed over us. The soft, ambient lighting cast a gentle glow, and our enthusiasm echoed throughout the room.

I took charge and suggested some quirky activities we could enjoy in Clarkston. This was not an investigation trip but a chance to bond and create new memories.

"Alright, ladies," I began, a playful glint in my eye, "I've got three quirky Clarkston experiences lined up for us. Let's choose one to make our day memorable. Option one," I continued, "we can attend one of Clarkston's famous outdoor movie nights in the town square. Picture this, cozy blankets, a picnic basket with our favorite snacks, and a classic film under the starry night sky. It's a charming way to enjoy a cinematic adventure."

After I revealed the first option, my friends exchanged excited glances.

Breanna said, "That sounds magical, Samantha! I imagine us snuggled up with blankets, watching an old classic. Count me in for option one."

Holli added with a grin, "I'm with Breanna on this. I'm all for it. Plus, it's a chance to show off my picnic basket-packing skills."

Rebeccah nodded saying, "I'm in too. Watching a film under the stars sounds like a dream. Let's do it!"

It was unanimous and no need to discuss the others. I couldn't help but share in their enthusiasm. It was settled; our evening would be spent enjoying a cinematic adventure under the Clarkston night sky.

With a thoughtful expression, I began, "Alright, ladies, before we dive into our fun activity, we need to establish a clear game plan for our investigation. We must be systematic and thorough to uncover the truth about Hope for Tomorrow's issues. Here are some initial strategies we can consider."

Breanna leaned forward, and I continued, "First, let's gather as much information as possible about the organization's recent activities and finances. We'll request their most recent financial reports and records. This will help us identify any irregularities or discrepancies."

Holli nodded in agreement. I added, "I think it's also crucial that we speak to current and former employees or volunteers who might have insights into the organization's operations. They might provide us with valuable information about potential organizational issues."

Rebeccah chimed in, and her perspective was valuable: "We should reach out to Hope for Tomorrow's programs and services beneficiaries. Their experiences and feedback may find any problems. It's essential to understand how these issues affect everyone."

The sun began to dip below the horizon, casting a warm orange glow across the Clarkston sky. We gathered our snacks for our night under the stars. We found a cozy spot and lay our blankets in a circle. The lawn felt cool and dewy beneath us, offering a refreshing contrast to the warmth of the evening.

The giant screen was set against a backdrop of tall trees, and as the first stars began to twinkle overhead, the screen flickered to life. The excitement was contagious, and the surroundings came alive with the magic of the cinema.

Time slipped away as we lost ourselves, and when the credits rolled, we sat there, taking in the serenity. The night under the stars had been a resounding success, a memory we would cherish for years.

Breanna, her eyes still shimmering with the movie's enchantment, turned to us with a grin. "This is incredible. I haven't had such a night in ages," she mused.

Holli, who had enjoyed the snacks just as much as the film, said, "And this setting? Perfect. Samantha, you can pick the best experiences in your new town."

I nodded, my heart warmed by the joy of the evening. "I'm so glad we got to experience this together."

We packed up our picnic with smiles and hearts full of contentment, knowing that our Clarkston adventure had just begun.

Chapter 5

My concerns regarding possible corruption remained a persistent source of unease. The weight of responsibility as a board member bore down on me. I oversaw the organization's economic well-being and integrity, and the looming suspicion of fraud burdened my conscience.

There was also a personal dimension to this ordeal. The organization's mission, empowering underprivileged youth, resonated with me. The mere thought that funds meant to uplift these vulnerable individuals could be misused or stolen filled me with profound disappointment and sadness. I was torn between the desire to avoid premature conclusions and the need to address the evident warning signs. This internal struggle persisted, fueled by the fear of likely repercussions from unfounded allegations.

Holli and I delved into the labyrinth of the organization's records, a task we perfected over time. Our synergy in navigating documents was seamless. Holli was a seasoned legal expert with a sharp mind. She was meticulous and had a no-nonsense approach to the case. Her arranged black hair framed her face, and her piercing blue-green eyes never missed details.

My role was concentrating on the fiscal papers and inspecting agreements with various entities. My attention was unwavering. My reputation was the ability to unravel complex puzzles, and I often lost track of time when thinking.

I stumbled upon several that lifted my eyebrows. Cross-referencing the dealings with contractual obligations only intensified our doubts. One discovery stood out: a sequence of disbursements made to a company unrelated to the nonprofit's mission and operations. The payments were substantial and lacked a discernible purpose or legitimate justification. I delved deeper, and a troubling connection emerged—the recipient company had ties to a close confidant of Mr. Tampani.

"This is irregular," I remarked, my concern evident. There's no justifiable reason for the nonprofit to make the disbursements. It appears to be a covert method of diverting funds to someone linked with the CEO."

My discovery injected complexity into the inquiry, unveiling the CEO's and his associates' possible involvement in fraudulent, deceitful behavior. Emotions ran high as I realized the gravity of the situation. My expertise and unwavering attention to detail proved essential in illuminating the questionable dealings, solidifying our growing belief that misconduct might unfold. Throughout this process, I stayed resolute in my commitment to objectivity and meticulousness, ensuring that every proof I uncovered was ironclad.

Holli's acknowledgment of the significance of our findings brought a sense of validation and purpose. "The details we need to move forward," she affirmed. "Clear proof of abnormalities will be instrumental in presenting a compelling case to the board and the authorities."

Her words resonated with me, filling me with relief and motivation. "Thank you," I responded.

The clues we unearthed reinforced our suspicions and strengthened our confidence. My ability to decipher complex documents and spot red flags proved invaluable. I trust in Holli's expertise in navigating the legal intricacies of our research. Together, we forged ahead with a steadfast resolve to uncover the truth and ensure justice prevailed.

I spoke up, my voice carrying eagerness. "I've got some perceptions on those files. They trace back to a company known as Sparkling Clean Solutions and Sarai Bennett, who serves as the Finance Manager."

Breanna and Rebeccah sat huddled around my dining table. Their eyes were framed by glasses, and she scrutinized each piece of proof with laser-like precision.

Their expressions of tenacity as they pored over the messages I provided. The digital trail of communications was a promising goldmine of facts.

Breanna sorted the electronic mail, categorizing them by sender and date. Her brow furrowed as she scanned each message to identify patterns and inconsistencies. Rebeccah focused on cross-referencing the email content with other documents they obtained.

She turned, "We need to start setting up interviews with the individuals mentioned in these communications. There are too many connections here to ignore."

Rebeccah nodded, her gaze fixed on the screen. "You're right. The more people we talk to, the clearer the picture becomes. Let's begin with the most critical ones."

Breanna and Rebeccah prepared to meet with Sarai Bennett and Josh Williams of Sparkling Clean Solutions. They uncovered crucial information about questionable dealings. They recognized the importance of speaking with board members Emily Raymond and

Bobby Guzman to gain insights into their recent argument. I suggest contacting Dakota to gauge whether he possesses any pertinent details. We needed to tread cautiously to avoid arousing suspicion as we continued our examination.

They outlined the essential questions they would pose during these gatherings. They aimed to delve into the records, scrutinizing the legitimacy of invoices and transactions directed toward Sparkling Clean Solutions under Josh Williams's ownership. They knew that comprehending the full scope of the contract was pivotal in uncovering any irregularities.

Rebeccah and Breanna prepared to depart for an appointment with Sarai Bennett and Josh Williams. Their burning desire to unearth critical findings into the organization's intricacies fueled their footsteps, driving them forward with the misgivings gripping them all.

We examined the records, revealing inconsistencies that hinted at hidden funds and concealed assets. These red flags indicated something needed fixing inside the organization's economic landscape. Questionable expenditures with unfamiliar vendors and offshore accounts painted a troubling picture.

We continued analyzing the data. The enigmatic riddle of anomalies demanded our unwavering attention. Holli and I were a well-synchronized team, combining my analytical skills with her keen eye for detail. Each piece of data we examined revealed complicated threads of the organization's situation.

We discovered a wealth of knowledge hidden within the electronic archives. The correspondence I flagged turned out to be a goldmine of proof. We sifted through the electronic message and uncovered a web of deceit and deception.

We discovered interaction between Dakota and several individuals with unfamiliar names. The individuals were involved in dealings shady at best. Disbursements to obscure offshore accounts were documented, and invoices that appeared to be fictitious were exchanged. The messages hinted at a complex money laundering scheme that the CEO and his associates were orchestrating.

We sifted through the exchange and stumbled upon a thread of electronic mail that caught our attention. They weren't your typical business notes but cryptic and shrouded in secrecy. Mentions of "off-the-record" gatherings and rendezvous at undisclosed locations awoke our curiosity.

I glanced at Holli, my brow furrowing. "Holli, take a look at this," I said, nodding towards the screen. "Electronic emails mention secretive private sessions, and they're being kept off the official record. What do you make of this?"

Holli's eyes scanned the screen, her expression mirroring my curiosity. "This is unusual," she remarked, her voice above a whisper. "The rest of the staff intentionally hid these gatherings. Why? Who's involved?"

My heart quickened as we stumbled upon references to secretive rendezvous hidden within the digital correspondence. The thrill of the discovery tempered a growing sense of unease, like a storm brewing on the horizon. My mind raced with questions. What were these meetings, and why were they kept off the official record? The secrecy around them hinted at something significant that may be crucial to unraveling the misconduct we were investigating.

Holli and I exchanged glances, unable to resist the urge to delve deeper.

"We can't ignore this," Holli whispered. "The secretive gatherings may be a key piece of the puzzle. They might hold the answers we've been searching for."

I nodded in agreement, and my pulse quickened. "We don't have enough data yet. We must gather more and determine who's been attending the sessions."

I stumbled upon a breakthrough. I found an email thread with a subject line that sparked my interest. The participants' names were concealed under aliases, but the content of the emails hinted at their true identities.

"Holli," I whispered. "I've found it. I know who's been in these secretive meetings." My voice quivered.

Holli's eyes met mine, her curiosity piqued. "Who is it? Who's been involved?" Her voice was calm, matching the gravity of the moment.

I leaned in closer, my fingers hovering over the keyboard, ready for the truth. "It's Tampani and some top-level executives. They've been assembling away from the organization files."

I was in disbelief because I witnessed Dakota's public persona. The man who advocated for the welfare of underprivileged youth, the face of an organization dedicated to a noble cause. This facade inspired trust and admiration in many, including myself. The stark contrast between this public image and the reality of his involvement in clandestine gatherings was almost too much to comprehend.

Disappointment engulfed me as I grappled with the stark betrayal of the organization's mission and the trust of those who placed their faith in Dakota. He had been a role model for the children, and the thought that he might be involved in something sinister shattered the ideals I held dear.

Anger simmered beneath the surface, directed at Dakota, and the circumstances that led to this revelation. How may someone who professed dedication to a noble cause engage in such deceit? My frustration boiled over at the injustice and the potential harm inflicted on the people Dakota vowed to protect.

My anger smoldered, and I found solace in Holli's unwavering commitment to the investigation. Her legal expertise illuminated the gravity of the situation, making it clear that the evidence we uncovered was more than just a collection of suspicious transactions; it was a trail leading straight to misconduct, with potential implications of embezzlement and fraud. The emails, once mere puzzle pieces, now formed a compelling narrative of wrongdoing.

Holli identified the legal implications. The emails provided a clear trail of questionable transactions that may not be explained as legitimate business activities.

My meticulous examination of the organization's digital records revealed discrepancies in the statements. These discrepancies hinted at hidden funds and undisclosed assets, suggesting a deliberate effort to conceal Hope for Tomorrow's economic status.

Holli and I pieced together the puzzle as we continued to work. We uncovered information about secretive meetings held off the organization's official record. One particular meeting, scheduled at an undisclosed location, raised suspicions. These were intentionally kept off the books, and their content was saved from the board or other staff members.

Intriguingly, we also stumbled upon anonymous tips submitted through the organization's internal reporting system. One tipster called themselves a "whistleblower" and claimed to have proof of wrongdoing within Hope for Tomorrow. This whistleblower, however, remained unidentified in the emails.

Holli and I discussed our findings. It became clear we were dealing with a complex web of unethical behavior within the organization. We unearthed substantial indications and knew it was time to take our discoveries to the board and authorities.

"We have a strong case here," Holli remarked, her voice tinged with determination. "The emails, financial discrepancies, and clues of secretive meetings all point to a concerted effort to hide financial improprieties. We should prepare a comprehensive report."

I nodded, my sense of responsibility deepening. "We can't forget about that whistleblower. We need to find out who they are. This may be the key to unraveling the entire scheme."

Holli and I communicated with Breanna and Rebeccah as the day passed. Short updates and occasional phone calls allowed us to exchange valuable insights from our tasks.

We awaited Rebeccah and Breanna's return from their meetings. An air of anticipation filled the room as we prepared to regroup and share the information we gathered. The clock continued its steady march, and I took a brief respite from our investigative work to prepare a homemade dinner for our team.

In the kitchen, the alluring scent of garlic and onions sizzling in olive oil filled the house, creating an inviting and comforting atmosphere. I stirred the chicken simmered in the creamy alfredo sauce, infusing it with flavor and depth. The aroma wafted around, embracing me in warmth and togetherness.

I added the finishing touches to our dinner, and Rebeccah and Breanna returned. Their expressions revealed their recent interview with Sarai Bennett and Josh Williams. Without delay, they began to share their experiences.

Breanna and Rebeccah sat across from me. They were eager to share the insights they gained.

Breanna's brown eyes sparkled with curiosity, and she pushed her glasses up her nose. Rebeccah, in contrast, exuded a calm, composed demeanor. Her auburn and wavy hair framed her face, and her striking blue eyes hinted at her sharp intellect. She had a penchant for jotting down notes during conversations.

Breanna's eyes lit up as she began, "She was forthcoming and shared some vital knowledge. We mentioned the transactions and discrepancies. She acknowledged that some inconsistencies have also elevated her doubts."

I leaned forward. "Tell me more," I urged.

Rebeccah said, "Sarai confirmed that she noticed the same things. There were concerns in her department."

Breanna added, "She pointed out specific deals that lacked clear explanations or documentation. These included payments to unfamiliar vendors, which caught her attention as problematic."

My mind raced as I processed these facts. It was a significant breakthrough, confirming wrongdoing in Hope for Tomorrow.

There was more. Rebeccah continued, "She mentioned that she received unusual appointment requests from the CEO, Josh Williams. These meetings were kept off the official record, and their content was not shared with the finance team or other staff members. This secrecy triggered red flags for her."

Breanna said, "During our discussion with Josh Williams, we learned more about the cleaning and sanitation services they provide. We inquired about the invoices and payments, and he understood the scope of their contract with the non-profit. We couldn't find any direct connection between him and Tampani."

Holli asked, "Did Josh mention unusual or undocumented transactions in their dealings? Anything that might raise concerns?"

Rebeccah considered before responding, "No, he didn't mention anything irregular in their business deals or agreements. Their contract appears to have been straightforward regarding services and payments."

These details didn't immediately point to monetary impropriety. Understanding the organization's contracts and vendors was essential. We needed to explore every lead and follow any potential trails.

I began to inform the others about a discovery I made while examining Hope for Tomorrow's reports. A name caught my attention—Makenzie. She had been a part of the accounting department a year ago but left without specifying a reason. The timing of her departure struck me as questionable. A nagging thought began to form in my head: Could she be a crucial witness with insights into the differences and the connections we were seeking?

I shared my observation regarding Makenzie's departure, and Breanna's eyes widened in surprise. "Wait, could this be the same Makenzie we encountered at the coffee shop?" she inquired, her voice carrying a hint of curiosity.

"It's a possibility," I responded, my thoughts racing. "I hadn't connected the dots earlier, but now that you mentioned it, there's a chance it's the same woman. We should explore this further."

It was time to delve deeper into this newfound connection and uncover the reasons behind Makenzie's abrupt departure as the executive assistant of Hope for Tomorrow. Breanna and Rebeccah devised a plan to speak with employees who worked with her, hoping to unearth the circumstances surrounding her exit from the non-profit.

We embarked on this investigative path, and a slew of questions arose. Could Makenzie's resignation be linked to the suspected economic discrepancies, suggesting her knowledge of or involvement in dubious actions? Alternatively, was her departure unrelated to the current predicament? These inquiries provoked more uncertainties than they provided answers.

Each revelation showed that Makenzie might possess valuable knowledge of the organization's inner workings. Her departure added another layer of complexity to our inquiry. It deciphered her perspective, and her potential role would prove pivotal to uncovering the truth.

Holli chimed in, adding another piece to the puzzle. "We also came across the name of a former employee, Jessica Numan, who pressed concerns about the organization's fiscal management. Jessica had a substantial tenure with the organization and rose to a significant position in the accounting department. Her dedication and efficiency were well-regarded among her colleagues."

Jessica's time at the non-profit ended a few months before I joined the Board of Directors. According to the official statement, she resigned for personal reasons, and the organization conveyed its best wishes for her future endeavors. "People leave their jobs for various reasons," I added, acknowledging the diversity of circumstances that could lead to such decisions.

I suggested a plan of action. "I believe it would be wise for Breanna and Rebeccah to arrange an interview with Jessica tomorrow. Holli and I can visit the coffee shop to see if we can gather more details from Makenzie."

Everyone agreed, and Breanna lightened the mood, declaring, "Let's go eat!"

We gathered around the dining table, and my phone buzzed. I assumed it might be a message from Seth inquiring about my day and our plans.

The first message read: "Stop digging into things that don't concern you. This is your final warning."

Disturbing news greeted me. The sender's identity stayed shrouded in mystery, as the number was unfamiliar. My heart quickened, and the atmosphere in the room grew tense.

I attempted to dismiss the text as intimidation tactics. However, the anonymous sender's knowledge of our ongoing inquiry and persistent attempts to deter us raised troubling questions about the extent of the fraud.

I shared the threatening text with my friends, who mirrored my concerns. Rebeccah was the first to vocalize her unease, her voice tinged with worry. "This is unsettling," she remarked.

I tried to trace the source, but they seemed to originate from a burner phone, rendering it challenging to identify the sender. Breanna's eyes narrowed with suspicion as she analyzed the situation. "Whoever is behind this has a desire to halt our progress. They're resorting to a threat. It's a sign we're on the right track. We must exercise heightened vigilance and caution in our analysis."

Holli nodded, her expression resolute. "You're right. We must remain focused and continue gathering details. The individual behind these notes likely has ties to the fraud."

Aware of the need for discretion and caution, we agreed to maintain silence about the threats as we drew closer to uncovering the truth. We recognized the importance of our safety and vowed to watch each other's backs, ensuring we kept sharp and persistent in the days ahead.

Chapter 6

A gnawing sense of unease accompanied my every thought as I awoke on another restless morning. I couldn't shake the unsettling notion that Tampani might indeed be embroiled in the fraudulent activities we were uncovering. It was an alarming idea, and a part of me struggled to accept it. How might someone who presented himself as a champion of underprivileged youth be behind such deceit?

I reached for my laptop, intent on delving again into the digital footprint we dissected in the previous days. The soft glow of the screen illuminated my face as I revisited the questionable emails that initiated our examination. The digital paper trail was a complex labyrinth.

I scrutinized the electronic mail further and discovered a new thread that led me deeper into the narrative of fraud and deception.

I took a deep breath, my voice steady but laden with the gravity of the situation. "There's something I need to discuss," I began, my eyes darting between my friends. "During my early morning digital research, I stumbled upon another name—Emily Raymond. Emily might be connected."

The mention of Emily Raymond concerning questionable deals sent a jolt of surprise through my veins. Emily was a fellow director, and the thought of their involvement was both shocking and unsettling.

Breanna and Rebeccah swapped worried looks, and their expressions mirrored my turmoil. The room fell silent, broken only by the distant hum of morning traffic outside.

"Emily Raymond? That's unexpected." Breanna spoke, her voice laced with concern. "We need to find out more, but we must tread carefully. We need more proof."

Rebeccah nodded, her analytical mind already at work. "Agreed. Samantha, do you think it's wise for Breanna and me to visit Emily, Bobby Guzman, and Jessica Numan today? We should inquire about any facts they might have regarding the recent tensions among the members."

After our discussion, we made plans to split up for the time being and reconvene later for dinner. They hopped into Rebeccah's car to interview Emily, Bobby, and Jessica. Hoping Breanna and Rebeccah would unearth something to vindicate Dakota.

Holli and I embarked on our journey to visit Makenzie. We walked into the coffee shop, and the aroma of brewed coffee filled the air, mingling with the sweet scent of pastries. Artwork adorns the walls. The owner curated a collection of paintings and photographs, creating an artistic and dynamic space.

I recognized Makenzie behind the counter, attending to customers, taking orders, and preparing drinks. I traded looks with Holli and gave Makenzie space to finish her tasks before approaching her. Makenzie looked up from behind the counter, her face lighting up with surprise and a touch of apprehension as she recognized us. "Hi, how can I help you today?" she asked, maintaining her composure.

"We just wanted to talk, Makenzie," I said, hoping to put her at ease. "Mind if we sit down for a moment?"

"Sure," Makenzie answered, wiping her hands on her apron and motioning towards a corner table.

I noticed the nervousness in her eyes. "Makenzie, we understand you used to receive assistance from Hope for Tomorrow," I began, letting her reveal we understood her connection to the organization.

Her eyes softened. "Yes, they helped my family when we were going through a tough time," she admitted, conveying emotion. "I have a younger sister, and things were rough back then."

Holli nodded, encouraging Makenzie to continue. "It's not easy to ask for help, but it can make all the difference," she said empathetically.

Makenzie glanced around, checking if anyone was eavesdropping. "Yeah, it did. It's been a while since then, and I thought I was in a good place. Thanks to the owner giving me a chance, I got a job here."

I sensed more of her story, so I probed further. "Is there something else, Makenzie? Something might be bothering you?"

Her eyes welled up with tears, and she looked down, composing herself before speaking again. "My daughter was supposed to be involved in the afterschool program, and now she can't, and finding quality childcare I can afford is next to impossible. I don't want to bring her here, but what else can I do? I wanted her to have the same opportunities I did when I was younger. There's no funding for the program anymore."

I glanced at Holli, understanding the weight of Makenzie's words. I commented. "We're trying to ensure the organization continues to support families like yours. Makenzie, we must determine if something more is happening here."

She hesitated, torn between her loyalty to the workplace and her desire to help us. "I can't say much," she said, her voice above a whisper. "Mr. Tampani, he's not the person he pretends to be. Something is going on."

Holli leaned in, "We believe you. We think some activities might happen, and we need your help to find the truth."

Her eyes widened. "Ok, how can I help?" she asked, her voice trembling.

"If you know anything that can help, it could make a significant difference," Holli commented.

She confessed she worked for Hope for Tomorrow. "During my time as Tampani's executive assistant, I spotted him in and out of the office, and mysteriously, something didn't seem right. I decided to speak with him, hoping he would address my worries and provide some clarity." Makenzie continued, "He dismissed my concerns and discouraged me from looking further into the matter. Seeing my worries brushed aside when I only wanted to ensure everything was honest was disheartening."

Holli leaned forward, her expression empathetic, and asked, "Can you give us an example of any transactions raising red flags for you?"

She nodded, grateful for their understanding, and said, "I came across invoices that didn't have any basis or relation to the organization's operations. They appeared fictitious or inflated, and it troubled me. I tried to investigate further, but I faced resistance and hostility from some of my colleagues. It was as if they didn't want anyone questioning what was happening."

Holli's eyes narrowed with concern, and she inquired, "And how did that make you respond?"

"I was overwhelmed," she admitted, "and realizing my ethical values compromised was disheartening. It became clear that something wasn't right within the organization, and I realized I couldn't stay in such an environment any longer."

I reached out, placing a comforting hand on her shoulder, and said, "Makenzie, we admire your courage in speaking up about this. Your insights are invaluable, and we're here to support you every step of the way."

Makenzie was lost in thought, her gaze drifting to a corner where a young girl sat with schoolbooks spread across the table. At around eight years old, her dark, silky hair cascaded in gentle waves, framing her cherubic face like a halo. The sights and sounds faded as she shared her story. Her voice trembled with emotion as she spoke, "Everything is all about her. She is my daughter." The tenderness and vulnerability in her words touched our hearts. We witnessed the pride in her eyes as she glanced at the young girl in the corner.

Rebeccah smiled, offering support, "Makenzie, your daughter is lucky to have you as her mother."

She looked up at us. "I've had a troubled past," she began. "There were many struggles I had to overcome."

"What concerns you most about Dakota's behavior?" I asked gently, sensing the weight of her words.

Makenzie hesitated; the look on her face let us know she was overwhelmed with emotions. She voiced a more profound fear.

"It's impacting my daughter's future," Makenzie confessed. "I'm worried about what this means for her."

"We're here to protect Hope for Tomorrow," Holli assured her. "Our goal is to ensure its mission continues."

Makenzie nodded, taking a deep breath. "When I was Tampani's executive assistant, it became clear I couldn't stay. I wasn't involved in the fraud. I resigned because I wouldn't compromise my values or work in such a toxic environment."

Her voice wavered as she continued, "It hurt to leave, but I had to do what was best for my daughter and me."

I reached out and touched her hand. "You made a brave choice. We respect that."

The conversation shifted to personal reflections, and Makenzie's raw emotions were evident. We listened, feeling a deep empathy for her situation.

After a while, we said our goodbyes and stepped outside. The sounds of the coffee shop faded, replaced by the city's ambient noises. The scent of coffee clung to our clothes, reminding us of our meaningful discussion.

As we walked away, Holli turned to me. "She's been through so much. I respect her courage."

"Me too," I replied. "We understand her perspective now, which will help us move forward."

My phone vibrated. I glanced at the screen and spotted Breanna's name. I opened the message.

Breanna's text read: "Meeting with Emily went well. She was concerned about the recent issues and said she might have some info to share. We're headed to Bobby Guzman's place now."

I shared the update with Holli, her eyes widening with hope and anticipation.

I typed a response to Breanna's message: "Good news about Emily. I'll need more details later to confirm everything. I want to emphasize that Makenzie is not involved. Our discussion with her today made it clear."

My primary concern is vindicating Makenzie and shielding her from any unwarranted suspicions in this unraveling scandal.

As we headed back to the house for further forensics work, I had an idea. I turned to Holli.

"Let's pay Dakota a visit in person."

"Sounds like a good plan," she agreed. "Do you think he'll be available?"

I smiled, "Of course! I'm his favorite new member."

I dialed Dakota's number. The phone rang twice before a voice answered on the other end, curious and inquiring, "Hello, who's calling?"

"This is Samantha Donavan."

"Hello, Samantha!" Dakota, on the other end, was warm and welcoming. "How can I help you?"

"Hi, I was wondering if you might have some time to chat with my friend Holli and me."

"Sure thing," Dakota responded. "Come on by. Anything for my favorite new board member."

I shot Holli a triumphant look and grinned. "Okay, we'll be there in 20."

"Meet you soon, Samantha," he replied before hanging up the phone.

Turning to Holli, I couldn't resist a playful wink. "I told you I was his favorite."

Holli and I drove to Dakota's house. "Let's hope our chat with him unveils some facts," I said.

Holli and I pulled up to the house, and a knot of anticipation tightened in my stomach. The elegant exterior of his home stood in stark contrast to the turbulent suspicions that brought us here. The house exuded an air of affluence, its grandeur evident in the stately columns framing the entrance. The pristine and wide driveway could accommodate several cars.

I glanced at Holli, her gaze reflecting the same interest. He greeted us at the door, his welcoming smile belying the guarded demeanor lurking beneath the surface. His tailored suit and confident posture were familiar, but now they had an enigmatic quality that made me question everything I thought I knew about him.

"Hello, Samantha and Holli," he said, his voice smooth and composed. I'm glad you could make it. Please come in." Dakota held the door open.

We engaged in polite small talk, discussing inconsequential matters. After a delicate pause, I broached the subject that brought us here. "Dakota," I began, my voice steady but tinged with earnestness, "we wanted to discuss some concerns we've encountered regarding the organization, the recent discrepancies, and emails."

Dakota's eyes flickered, and a veil of guardedness descended over his countenance. "I see," he responded, his tone measured, "What exactly have you come across?"

The conversation took a turn as we delved into the heart of the matter. Holli and I posed questions, seeking answers and clarification about the allegations that overshadowed Hope for Tomorrow.

"Samantha and I have noticed some discrepancies in the financial records," said Holli. "Can you explain why certain expenses don't match the income statements?"

Dakota leaned back in his chair, a slight frown on his face. "I assure you, everything is accounted for. Sometimes there are delays in recording transactions, but that doesn't mean there's anything wrong."

I exchanged a meaningful glance with Holli, then asked, "What about the emails we've found? They suggest that some board members might be involved in unauthorized transactions."

He shifted uncomfortably. "Those emails are taken out of context. You have to understand there are always misunderstandings in communication. We're a large organization; not everyone is privy to the full picture."

Holli pressed for details, her tone becoming more insistent. "Can you give us specifics about these misunderstandings? And what about the involvement of certain board members? Their names appear repeatedly in these questionable transactions."

Dakota's eyes narrowed slightly, and he spoke carefully. "The board members you're referring to are highly respected. Any allegations against them are unfounded. We've conducted our internal reviews, and everything checks out."

His responses often danced around the core issues, showing denial, deflection, and explanations, which raised more questions than they answered. The room had an undeniable undercurrent of tension as we listened, our expressions combining scrutiny and polite engagement.

"Thank you for your time, Dakota," I said as our meeting ended. "We appreciate your willingness to discuss these concerns."

He stood up, a strained smile on his face. "Of course. If you have any more questions, don't hesitate to reach out."

We bid him farewell and walked from the elegant foyer to the front door. Once outside, Holli and I exchanged a knowing look.

"Well, that was enlightening," Holli remarked dryly.

We both rolled our eyes. "Definitely," I agreed. "There's more to this than he's letting on."

We both laughed, though deep down, I realized our encounter with Dakota hadn't yielded our sought-after answers. His responses had been as evasive as I anticipated, cloaking any potential truth in vague promises and assurances everything was "for the children." Beneath those well-practiced words, I sensed a hidden layer, a secret he was guarding.

I gripped the steering wheel, my knuckles turning white. Dakota was concealing something, and whether it related to the potential fraud or another undisclosed issue, we needed to uncover it.

My phone buzzed, causing my heart to skip a beat. It could have been another threatening message. I reached for the phone and glanced at the screen. To my relief, it was a text from Seth.

It read, "I will be home soon. We caught the bad guys early. How is everything going? I can't wait to listen to it. You four are great; you'll find all you need quickly. Love you!"

Holli inquired, her eyes filled with intrigue, "Good news?"

I met Holli's gaze and smiled, a sense of joy and relief bubbling within me. "This is the best news a girl could ask for," I answered.

Holli and I made our way back home. Our meeting with Dakota yielded some details and raised more questions. I couldn't help but wonder about the secrets he was holding, whether they were related to the allegations or something else.

A peculiar sight greeted us. A box was sitting on the front porch. It wasn't something I had been expecting. My heart quickened with fascination and caution. We traded looks, and Holli's brows furrowed in contemplation.

"Did you order something?" Holli asked, her voice calm and concerned.

I shook my head, my eyes fixed on the unassuming package. "No, I didn't. This is unexpected."

We approached the doorstep, and I picked up the container. It was wrapped and had no return address. My emotions ranged from interest to a slight unease. What could this contain, and who left it here?

I opened the package, revealing its contents. Inside, we found a collection of documents, photographs, and a handwritten note. The pictures depicted various scenes from Hope for Tomorrow's events, and the papers seemed to be financial records.

Holli and I were engrossed in examining the contents of the mysterious delivery when our phones rang, jolting us out of our focused concentration.

I answered the call, and Breanna's voice came through the speaker, tinged with a hint of disappointment and frustration. "Samantha, Holli, it's us. We've just wrapped up our meeting with Bobby Guzman." The eagerness was intense as we listened, hoping for a breakthrough. Breanna continued, "I'm sorry there wasn't much we could gather from him. He denied any knowledge of the financial differences."

Holli's brows furrowed with a combination of disappointment and concern. We hoped Bobby might have details, but our efforts had failed him.

Breanna continued, "And as for Jessica, she confirmed she worked at Hope for Tomorrow for a specific period, but beyond that, she didn't have much insight into the recent events or the alleged misconduct."

Rebeccah said, her voice reflecting a similar disappointment, "It's like we're facing a wall here, Samantha. We need more concrete facts or someone to step forward and be willing to provide knowledge."

"I think you should come back to the house," I said, excitement bubbling. "We've received a little unexpected present left at the doorstep."

"Really?" Rebeccah chimed in, her curiosity piqued. "I can't wait to see what it contains."

I added, "We could use some help playing Connect the Dots. You know what they say: Four heads are better than two."

"Okay, we'll be there in 15 minutes," Breanna said. "Do you want me to pick something up for dinner?"

"No need," I responded with a grin. "I'll just order a pizza and have it delivered. How does everyone think about pepperoni and pineapple?" I asked.

A chorus of "yes" echoed from everyone.

With the pizza on its way and the anticipation building, Holli and I were eager to delve into the contents of the mysterious package. It seemed hopeful in our exploration, a potential breakthrough in a case that felt like a dead end for far too long.

The sound of a car pulling into the driveway broke the stress. We rushed to the window and saw Breanna and Rebeccah stepping out of their vehicle. In a moment they were at the door.

"Come on in," I greeted them.

Holli laid the documents on the counter, and we learned to study the pages. We hoped the package's contents would help with our investigation.

Rebeccah spoke up first. "Let's start sorting these papers by date," she suggested. "Establishing a timeline might help us see patterns or connections."

Breanna broke the silence, her voice laced with concern. "It seems the one name that keeps coming up is Emily."

I nodded, my fingers tracing the lines of the records before me. "I understand. I cross-referenced these documents and viewed less of Dakota and more of Emily, which is still disturbing. I don't know what to think anymore."

Holli chimed in. "We need to stick to the evidence and search everything."

The doorbell rang, a welcome interruption to our intense discussion. "I bet that is the pizza," I said with a hint of relief as I reached into my purse for a tip for the delivery driver. I opened the door, and the aroma of baked pizza wafted in, filling the room with its irresistible scent.

We savored the slices of pizza, and the mood in the room shifted from tense to more relaxed. The flavors of pepperoni and pineapple danced on our taste buds, providing a reprieve from the complexities of our probe. Our talk flowed seamlessly between bites, each offering insights and theories as we attempted to connect the dots.

Breanna, her brow furrowed in concentration, initiated the discussion. "I can't shake the sensation that Emily holds the key to all this. There's just something about her involvement that doesn't make sense."

Holli nodded. "I've been going through fiscal records, and clear irregularities exist. We still need concrete evidence to tie everything together."

I added, "Makenzie's details about Dakota's behavior and concerns about inflated invoices could be a starting point. We might have a breakthrough if we find a paper trail linking these suspicions to Emily or anyone else."

"Let's focus on Emily for now." Rebeccah suggested, "Samantha, can you gather more facts regarding her economic connections with Hope for Tomorrow? Breanna, can you arrange another interview with her?"

Breanna nodded, determined. "Yes, I'll see if she's willing to share more."

"Let's get some sleep. I have a feeling tomorrow will be quite eventful," I suggested. We all nodded in agreement and headed to our separate rooms.

Chapter 7

In the next few days, our probe took us deeper into potential danger. Anonymous texts and calls began to increase and reach us, warning us to back off and leave the matter alone. We started receiving threatening emails and posts on social media.

The perpetrators went to great lengths to hide their identities, using fake accounts and encrypted messages to ensure autonomy. They implied that harm may come if we didn't abandon our ways. We discovered strange packages and letters left at the doorstep to intimidate us further. These packages contained warning symbols and secret notes, leaving us vulnerable and uneasy.

Holli, Rebeccah, Breanna, and I gathered in my living room to discuss our next steps.

"I can't believe these threats," Breanna said, looking worried. "This is getting serious."

"We need to be careful," Rebeccah added, rechecking her phone. "They mean business."

"I agree," Holli leaned forward. "But we can't back down now. We're close."

"What do you think we should do next?" I asked, trying to stay calm. "We can't let them scare us."

Rebeccah nodded. "We need to document everything. Every text, call, and email. It's all evidence."

"I'll handle the social media threats," Breanna said, her voice determined. "I'll report them and keep a record."

Seth said, "Samantha, I understand this is important to you, but your safety comes first. I don't want anything to happen to you or anyone else."

Breanna's fingers drummed on the table as the conversation continued in the living room. Breanna spoke, "Guys, we can't ignore the fact that this situation has escalated. The texts warn that someone wants us to back off. We need to be careful and consider the risks we face."

Holli chimed in, her tone solemn, "I agree with Breanna."

My voice unwavering, "We don't realize who we're dealing with here. Going to the authorities can provide us with the necessary protection and resources."

"You're right, Samantha. Our safety should come first. We've come so far, and handling this situation is essential." Rebeccah said.

Breanna added, "I'm worried about the risks, but we can't let fear stop us from doing what's right. Let's go to the authorities and team up with them."

Seth looked at me with love and worry. "I support you, Samantha, and I admire your persistence. Promise me you'll be careful and take all necessary precautions."

When we entered the police station lobby, the atmosphere transformed. Subdued lighting bathed the space in a muted glow, dampening any sound that dared to break the silence. The ornate molding on the ceiling offered subtle hints about the building's storied past. We moved forward into the heart of the station, ready to make our case.

Seth stopped in the lobby. "I will wait for you here. You go ahead."

I looked back at him. "Ok, honey. It shouldn't take long."

Detective John Mercer greeted us with a firm handshake and a no-nonsense expression. His eyes were sharp and observant, scanning the surroundings for signs of danger. His presence commanded respect.

"Good evening," Mercer said, his voice steady. "I understand you have some serious concerns."

"Yes," I began. "I am Samantha Donavan, and we have been looking into some financial issues with Hope for Tomorrow. We've received threats, including anonymous texts, calls, emails, and social media posts."

Holli handed over a folder. "We've documented everything," she said, " but we're worried for our safety."

Mercer opened the folder and quickly scanned the contents. "These are credible threats," he said. "You've done the right thing by coming here."

Rebeccah spoke up. "We believe it's connected to our investigation into 'Hope for Tomorrow.' There are hidden funds and possible fraud."

"Understood," Mercer said, his tone grim. "I'll need to ask you some detailed questions and take statements."

Breanna nodded. "We're ready to cooperate fully," she said. "We just want to make sure we're protected."

Mercer motioned for us to follow him. "Let's go to my office. We'll start with your statements and go from there."

We walked a short distance to his office, where we all sat, and he closed the door.

"Thank you for coming in," Mercer said, his voice smooth and reassuring, like the calming flow of a river. "I will review the proof you've brought in."

My friends and I exchanged glances.

"We did our best to gather as many details as possible," Breanna replied.

Holli chimed in. "We've found discrepancies in the financial reports that suggest possible embezzlement."

"We don't want the organization's good work to be tarnished by one person's actions." Rebeccah said.

I experienced a knot in my stomach. I tried to remain composed, speaking from the heart. "We stumbled upon something suspicious."

He also spotted Holli's beauty and looked right at her. "I appreciate your efforts," he said. "Fraud is a serious offense, and we will look into it. You've done the right thing by bringing this to our attention."

Leaving the police station, we conveyed our feelings to Detective Mercer and considered it a small victory.

Holli broke the silence, "It's a good start, but we can't rely on the police."

I added, "We need to protect ourselves from cyber risks. Our emails and texts may be monitored. We have to assume that our every move is being surveilled."

Seth, listening to our conversation, spoke up. "I might be acquainted with someone who can help with that. A friend from college works in cybersecurity. He's excellent at what he does."

The other women moved ahead toward the car, I came to a halt, my emotions evident from the stern expression on my face. I reached out to stop Seth, my gaze locking onto his with displeasure. "I don't want him involved." I asserted.

"Samantha," Seth began in a calm yet persuasive tone, "He's the best in the business. I understand there's tension between you two, but he is the best for this situation."

I realized he was right. "Fine, but here's the deal. You'll have to call him and tell him I haven't disclosed where I work to my friends. We'll need to develop a cover story for how we understand each other, at least until the time is right if it ever is."

"All right," Seth agreed, understanding the need for discretion. "I'll develop a cover story and keep you in the loop."

I sighed, "I hope I can handle working with him. He'll have to work remotely; we can't risk another person coming into town and telling anyone something's amiss."

Seth and I made it to the car as he drove, and I sat in the front passenger seat.

"We've made significant progress, but there's still one major hurdle in our path," Holli said. "The lack of concrete proof linking Dakota to the fraud is a significant challenge. We have suspicions and inconsistencies in the financial reports. We couldn't find any definitive proof of wrongdoing."

We settled on the oversized couch in my living room, surrounded by documents and notes. The room echoed with the sounds of our deep breaths.

Breanna was the first to break the uneasy quiet. "I can't shake the sensation that something more is happening here. The dangers we've received are too precise, too well-timed."

Rebeccah furrowed her brow in contemplation. "I've been thinking the same thing. It's like someone on the inside is feeding information to whoever's behind this."

The suspicion of a mole within Hope for Tomorrow had been hinted at, casting doubt. I sensed my stomach churn with anxiety and betrayal.

Seth glanced around the room, his gaze meeting each of his friends' troubled expressions. "This is serious, guys. If there's someone within the organization, it means we're not only dealing with externals."

Holli said, "How do we figure out who it might be? We can't point our fingers without proof."

Rebeccah leaned back in her chair, away from the documents she'd been reviewing, and rubbed her temples. "I've analyzed the financial records, cross-referenced emails, and interviewed some staff members. Nothing. It's like chasing shadows."

Breanna discovered a series of documents marked as "Confidential." She called the others over to her as she began to pull them up on a file. It looked like it was not encrypted and sent by email not too long ago.

Rebecca's voice reflected disbelief, "Hey, this is what we discussed with Bobby Guzman today. It's like a transcript of our conversation."

A sinking vibe settled in my stomach as I revealed, "This document originated from a meeting where he was present. I recall him jotting down notes."

Holli said, "Is it possible that Bobby is feeding someone insider details?"

We compared the notes from that session with the confidential document, and the gravity of the situation became undeniable. The level of detail documented mirrored his notes. There was an indisputable link between him and the facts leaked.

Breanna voiced the question that weighed on all our minds, "What drives his motives?"

I said, "That, my friends, is the million-dollar question."

"Let's not forget, we're dealing with much speculation here and no solid, concrete proof," Holli said.

Breanna commented, "We've come this far and can't let our perseverance waver now. We need to keep digging and finding new leads. There has to be something we've missed or overlooked."

We huddled together, poised to craft a plan to unveil Bobby's treachery and unmask the enigmatic recipient of his insider secrets.

Breanna's voice sliced through the heavy silence. "We must collect concrete facts that tie Bobby to these leaks. There can be no room for doubt."

Rebeccah added, "I propose we divide our efforts. Some delve into Bobby's activities, while the rest focus on unearthing the recipient's identity. Discretion is key. We cannot afford to tip our hand."

I leaned close to Seth and whispered, "All right, let's arrange a meeting with him tomorrow morning."

Chapter 8

S eth and I made a pact to rise early before the hustle and bustle of the day began. The anticipation of our private meeting with Mark weighed on us, and we understood the importance of discussing sensitive matters away from prying eyes and curious ears. The morning light struggled to pierce through the darkness outside; we were awake, eager to delve into the discussion.

He welcomed us into his hotel room. He closed the door behind him and greeted us hushed. "Seth, Samantha," he said, his voice carrying a confidentiality note, "I'm glad you made it."

Seth's gratitude needed no words; it was evident in his expression and sincerity of tone. "Mark," he began, "I can't express how much it means that you were here to watch Samantha while I was away. Your presence gave me peace of mind."

He nodded, his commitment to their safety unwavering. "You realize I've got your back."

I said, "Wait, you mean he has been in town this whole time, and you didn't tell me?"

Seth replied with regret, "I know what would have happened. You would have insisted he go home, saying you didn't need him around. I didn't want anything to happen to you while I was gone. You've received physical threats during this investigation, and your safety is my primary concern."

Admitting her fault, I turned to him. "You're right, and I probably would have told him to leave. You should have told me."

He conceded, "You're right. I should have told you."

I asked, "Since you've been watching me, can you identify the person who left the package on my doorstep?"

Mark replied, "Just show me a photo, and I can make an identification on the woman who was at your door."

"Her?" I asked, my curiosity piqued. "Give me a moment to find some photos." I reached for my phone and accessed my gallery. I began by showing him a picture of Makenzie.

He shook his head. "No, that's not her," he replied.

I moved on to the next one, showing him a picture of Emily.

Mark's response was the same. "No, it's not her either," he said.

With a sense of anticipation, I revealed the following picture.

"That's her. "I would recognize her anywhere." His words carried a note of conviction, revealing his confidence in the identification.

The picture unveiled the truth – Jessica left the package on my doorstep.

Seth looked at Mark and said, "Can you keep an eye on her and make sure she doesn't make another appearance at the house?"

"Of course!" Mark said.

Turning to him, I inquired, "Hey, do you think you can trace the origins of these phone messages? I have a strong hunch now, but I need an expert to examine the forensics and confirm my suspicions."

Mark nodded, his willingness to assist evident in his response. "Of course, Samantha. I'm here to help in any way I can."

"Thank you.", I responded.

Seth and I returned home, and a whirlwind of thoughts churned within me. It was a double-edged sword, shedding light on potential suspects while exonerating some individuals from our list of inquiries. It casts some doubt over Jessica's motives. It made me wonder if her focus on Dakota and Emily was a deliberate ploy to divert our attention from the perpetrator. These questions gnawed at my mind, demanding answers. We pulled up, and I was eager to ensure we were ready to move forward.

We all met in my living room, which became our go-to spot for brainstorming sessions and meaningful discussions. For breakfast, I brought a tray of pastries from a local bakery.

Rebeccah's eyes sparked, and her enthusiasm radiated. "I have an idea," she said. "What if we leverage the gala for our investigation?"

Her words seized our attention, drawing us closer as we awaited her proposal. "Picture an elegant and sophisticated event graced by influential community figures. It's the perfect cover. Everyone's focused on the glamour and the festivities. We can view Emily, Dakota, and anyone else involved," she added with a mischievous grin. "Did I mention my dress will be an absolute showstopper?"

Laughter rippled through the room, and grins bloomed on our faces. Holli chimed in, and her tone was unwavering and resolute. "Should we unearth any proof, it will be obtained within the bounds of legality and ethics."

The prospect of attending the gala thrilled us and presented an ingenious way to collect more proof. Rebeccah's eyes sparkled with enthusiasm as she described how we may investigate.

Rebeccah began, "We must ensure Emily is there. She's a central figure in all this, and her actions could reveal a lot."

Nods of agreement followed, and they all understood the importance of keeping a close eye on Emily throughout the event.

"Dakota," Holli chimed in, her voice laced with purpose. "He will more than likely be there. We need to have our stare on him. His interactions with people may tell us what he might be up to. It's our chance to watch him."

Breanna leaned forward, adding her perspective: "We should also have Bobby Guzman. If we monitor him, he might lead us to whom he is leaking the details."

I added, "Let's not forget Jessica. I received some news this morning, and I think she is not as innocent as she portrays herself."

Holli added, "We must comply with all the legal aspects of the evidence collecting. We can't afford any missteps, jeopardizing everything we have discovered and have it thrown out in court."

"Absolutely," I said, nodding. "We want to make sure we follow the rules on everything."

We spent hours planning and setting up the room to trap Tampani without arousing suspicion. Creating an environment that appeared natural and inviting while allowing us to spot suspicious behavior was essential.

"I have one responsibility for the gala," I said. "I am in charge of the seating chart." I was thinking about where to place our guests to optimize our efforts. We should seat our guests in areas that give us the best vantage point. It is crucial to position the surveillance."

Holli, always attentive to legal matters, raised an important question. "What about consent? We must ensure notification they are being taped."

Breanna, ever resourceful, offered a solution. "May we have them sign one when they arrive or post a sign?"

I considered the options. "Signs should be okay," I replied. "The tickets also state that they will be on camera.

I took charge of setting up the system. I installed small, hidden cameras in inconspicuous locations, such as behind potted plants and decorative items. They were state-of-the-art technology that allowed for high-quality video and audio recording. They were in place, and I connected them to a secure network I could access using my cellphone.

This way, I could monitor the live feed from my phone or laptop. I set up backup storage to ensure all the footage was recorded for later review. Holli ensured that everything we did was within the boundaries of the law. She reviewed Clarkston's privacy and surveillance laws, ensuring we were not infringing on anyone's rights while gathering proof.

We reviewed every contingency plan, ensuring we prepared for unexpected twists or turns. We were confident that our combined skills and expertise would lead us to success. We each had a person to observe. Rebecca would observe Bobby, Breanna Emily, Holli Dakota, and I would watch Jessica.

Later that night, I stepped into the exquisite venue for the fundraiser. The space was decorated with twinkling fairy lights that glowed and invited. Elegant floral arrangements graced each table, and banners displayed success stories of the children whose lives Hope for Tomorrow had touched. It was indeed a remarkable sight.

Breanna, Holli, and Rebeccah looked stunning in their elegant attire. Breanna wore a form-fitting gown in a rich shade of emerald, her fiery red hair cascading down her shoulders. Holli looked sophisticated in a tailored black dress, her black hair and blue-green eyes sparkling. Rebeccah exuded confidence in a chic navy-blue pantsuit in her impeccable style and red hair in a stylish updo. I decided on an elegant and contemporary look, donning a stylish black jumpsuit adorned with intricate beadwork.

The room buzzed with lively chatter and laughter as visitors mingled, sharing stories and experiences. Local business leaders and influential philanthropists were among the attendees, united by their support for the cause. Witnessing this gathering of people connected was heartwarming. Many contributed as donor volunteers or benefited from the organization's programs.

We became engrossed in conversations with the guests throughout the evening, conveying our profound gratitude for their unwavering dedication to the cause. Breanna and Rebeccah, with their exceptional charisma, moved through the crowd and captured those they conversed with.

The event continued, and she spotted Bobby sitting alone at a table. Rebeccah asked me to come over to his table with her. He was a tall, slender man with sharp features and combed, dark hair. She and I approached him for a talk, hoping to glean some information. She initiated the discussion, greeting him with a warm and friendly smile.

"Good evening," she greeted him. "I hope you're enjoying yourself."

He returned her smile. "Good evening. Yes, it's been quite an event. Everything has been impressive."

Rebeccah nodded. "It's been outstanding and heartwarming to witness the charity's impact on these talented young artists."

Bobby's eyes held a glimmer of curiosity. "It is. Are you involved with the organization?"

She maintained her friendly demeanor. "Yes, I'm a supporter, like many others here tonight. We believe in the cause."

I pulled out a chair and sat beside Rebeccah. "Bobby, we wanted to ask you a few financial questions."

He nodded, folding his hands on the table. "What do you need to know?"

Rebeccah leaned in slightly. "We've noticed some inconsistencies in the records. Have you seen anything unusual?"

Bobby sighed, glancing around. "No, I have not."

I exchanged a look with Rebeccah. "Nothing about hidden funds and strange transactions?"

He lowered his voice. "Nope."

Rebeccah nodded. "We need your help, Bobby. Any information you can share could be crucial."

He looked conflicted, then nodded slowly. "Anything to help you out, Samantha."

I gave him a reassuring smile. "Thanks, Bobby. We appreciate it."

Rebeccah and I got up from the table and went to a great vantage point in the room. We could see everyone.

I looked around and noticed Holli found herself in the company of Detective Mercer. They enjoyed each other's presence, her eyes twinkling and genuine smiles reflecting a budding friendship. With his rugged charm, Mercer appeared at ease in Holli's company, relishing her attention.

Breanna walked up to me with a big smile. She commented, "The food is incredible! The team outdid themselves with this gourmet spread. It's like a culinary masterpiece!"

I was beyond delighted with the food preparation's effort in bringing their culinary artistry to life. I praised their passion for creating a menu that catered to diverse palates and preferences. I marveled at their ability to balance flavors and textures, making each bite an unforgettable experience.

Breanna surveyed the lively crowd and detected Emily, who enjoyed herself as she engaged in animated conversations marked by smiles and laughter. She decided to approach her and went through with unwavering resolve.

Amidst the lively crowd, I watched the discussion, their expressions illuminated by a genuine grin. It became evident that something in the discussion surprised Emily. Her reaction was unmistakable—a subtle widening of her eyes, a slight shift in her posture. The atmosphere around them became animated, with Emily using expressive gestures, her arms and hands moving to emphasize her points. It was as if she was attempting to convey something significant. Her motions carried a sense of urgency.

Breanna appeared to be an attentive listener. Her response to Emily's explanation was subtle but indicative. I saw her nod, her body language conveying a sense of alignment with what she was hearing. It was a moment where words might have been unnecessary.

Breanna approached me, "Well," she began, her voice tinged with a hint of exasperation, "you can cross her off the list. She doesn't realize the depth of the financial reports or the expenditures made to various companies."

Holli, with a note of skepticism in her voice, asked, "Do you believe she's telling the truth?" She let out a heavy sigh, reflecting the weight of their situation.

She took a moment to consider her response, her brow furrowing in thought. "I think so," she replied, her tone conveying a sense of sincerity. "I understand all the facts point in her direction. I pressed her on some of the critical details, and she appeared clueless."

The entertainment for the evening was nothing short of spectacular. Harmony Soul took the stage, their instruments poised to serenade us with their musical tunes. The band's genre was a delightful blend of smooth jazz and soulful R&B, setting the perfect ambiance for the night. The group began to play, and their soothing melodies washed over the room like a gentle breeze, enveloping us in musical bliss. The soft and mellow tones blended seamlessly with the gala's warm and inviting atmosphere. It was like the music had its language, speaking to our hearts and souls and drawing us closer together.

The crowd swayed to the rhythm, and the melodic notes sometimes prompted some guests to join in and sing along. During the entertainment break, my gaze shifted toward Holli, who had her eyes fixed on Dakota. He moved through the room, going to each table and greeting the guests. His gestures were genuine as he shook hands and smiled. This was where he thrived, exuding charm and infectious enthusiasm. He shared his remarkable work in the Clarkston community.

Holli turned to me. "I believe we can rule out Dakota," she said, her gaze unwavering. "He's been circulating among the guests, spending no more than a minute or two with each person. He greeted everyone here. It doesn't fit the profile of someone harboring secrets."

I thought back to the meeting with Mark. Tampani is hiding a huge secret. One is costing him money, and one that would get ousted from his position as CEO. It was a secret I would reveal at the right time.

"I think you are right, Holli," I said. "I don't think he is involved in the fraud area."

My gaze fixed on Bobby as he made his way toward another figure. I glanced at Breanna, our eyes locking, and gestured toward Bobby's destination. It became clear that he was conversing with Jessica. Moments later, they scanned their surroundings before vanishing through a nearby side door. Breanna and I exchanged looks and headed towards the room housing the surveillance screens, tucked away just off the ballroom.

We notified Mercer, urging him to join us for observation. We turned our eyes to the screen. Our hearts sank at the sight of Jessica and Bobby locked in an embrace. A surge of questions filled our minds. Was this a romantic rendezvous? Always composed and strategic, he instructed us to return to the event to avoid arousing suspicion. Breanna and I complied, seamlessly blending into the ongoing program, our minds racing with uncertainty and intrigue.

The entertainment spotlight shifted from Harmony Soul to a group of talented young artists. These gifted performers had all been beneficiaries of Hope for Tomorrow's programs, and tonight, they graced us with their awe-inspiring talents. Their performances were captivating.

They took the stage, showing their artistic prowess through various art forms—singing, dancing, and even spoken word. It reminded us of all the greater purposes we served that night. Amidst the applause and cheers from the audience, we were humbled by the resilience and dedication displayed by these young artists. Their stories were a poignant reminder of the non-profit organization's impact on the lives of underprivileged youth.

After the children's performance, I turned to Rebeccah, witnessing the capable young artists on stage. With a broad smile, she looked at me and said, "Wow, incredible Sam! These kids are so talented and full of potential."

I nodded in agreement, still moved by the performances. "You're right. This is what it's all about—the impact we can have on these young lives. I feel so grateful to be a part of this organization and to have the opportunity to make a difference."

The event ended, and the air continued with a melodic symphony of sounds. Laughter and cheerful chatter intermingled with the gentle clinking of wine glasses, creating a harmonious ambiance that echoed through the room.

Turning to Holli, Breanna, and Rebeccah, I implored them to head to the control center and confer with Detective Mercer to glean his observations. They didn't pause, departing to carry out the task. I moved through the venue toward the exit to express my gratitude to the attendees. Among those leaving, I spotted Makenzie, who remained elusive throughout the night. Her eyes glistened with tears as she approached me, hinting at a concealed well of emotions.

Makenzie's voice quivered, her eyes welling up with tears as she began to speak. "I apologize for my absence tonight. It's just that. This event stirs up so many memories."

Sympathy filled my gaze, and I encouraged her to share more.

With a deep breath, she fought to regain her composure. "The success could change my family's life. It would mean my daughter could attend the after-school program instead of sitting alone in a corner at the coffee shop. I love having her around, but she needs to be with other children to have a structured learning environment after school. It could make all the difference."

Touched by the raw emotion in her words, I placed a reassuring hand on her shoulder. "I understand, and I promise your daughter will have the opportunity to join that program."

A faint, grateful smile crossed Makenzie's face. "I just wanted you to realize how much this organization means to families like mine."

Our heartfelt exchange made me thank her for attending and assure her that the Hope for Tomorrow community would embrace her daughter.

The attendees made their way out of the venue. They wore expressions of contentment and satisfaction. The captivating performances by the talented young artists left a profound impact on everyone's hearts. Their passionate singing, mesmerizing dance moves, and heartfelt spoken word performances touched a chord in the audience, reminding them of the power of Hope for Tomorrow's programs. Amidst the crowd, I caught glimpses of grins and tearful eyes.

Rebeccah, Breanna, and Holli returned to the room from the control booth. Their faces lit up with radiant smiles. Their expressions hinted at significant discoveries. Their animated gestures and the sparkles in their eyes told me they found something important. It was clear they were eager to share their newfound insights with me.

Holli mentioned, "We've been monitoring their interactions and conversations. So far, there haven't been any suspicious exchanges or behaviors from Emily or Dakota. They've been quite social, mingling with various visitors."

Rebeccah's eyes, dancing, leaned in and began, "Samantha, you won't believe what we found. We were monitoring the gala. We stumbled upon something intriguing. Bobby and Jessica had a private discussion, and Jessica pocketed an item from our placed bait."

Breanna chimed in, "Indeed, it wasn't just any item. One of our crafted baits is designed to lure anyone involved in fraudulent activities. Jessica's swift and deliberate actions suggest an intimate knowledge of our operations."

Holli added, "The full extent of this revelation remains uncertain, but it represents a significant breakthrough. Jessica's involvement may run deeper than our initial suspicions."

"We may have caught our fraudster," I remarked, unable to contain my satisfaction. "Let's return home, sleep on it, and reconvene in the morning. Holli, please invite Detective Mercer to meet with us in the morning. I have a hunch we're about to uncover some critical answers." I gave her a subtle wink.

Chapter 9

Breanna, Rebeccah, and Holli had convened in my living room, their expressions forming a mosaic of steely determination and captivating curiosity. The room was bathed in the soft, early morning light streaming through the windows, casting a delicate, almost ethereal luminescence over the space. Each group member had found a comfortable perch on plush couches and armchairs, their hands cradling steaming mugs of brewed coffee. The room resonated with a collective resolve, and our eyes held a shared determination.

We began discussing the previous night's discoveries. A sudden, jarring sound shattered the serene ambiance. The doorbell chimed, reverberations slicing through the calm like an urgent clarion call. Holli sprang to her feet, anticipating the visitor's identity. Mercer was standing there, his behavior composed and focused.

I smiled as she greeted him, "You are right on time, Detective. I was ready to disclose some details you might want to hear." Holli said.

"We all realize who the mole directors on the board of directors is. It was Bobby Guzman," I declared, my voice resonating with resolute conviction.

"Our fraudster is Jessica Numan!" Rebeccah exclaimed, her voice tinged with realization and anger. "They worked together to acquire inside facts."

"Exactly," I affirmed. "It became evident when we spotted them in the hallway together."

Mercer leaned in, his curiosity palpable. "She took the bait?"

"Hook, line, and sinker," Holli chimed in, her words laced with a hint of satisfaction as we reveled in the joy of putting the puzzle together.

Breanna leaned in, her eyes locked onto mine, brimming with determination that matched the gravity of our impending choice. "What's our next step? Should we confront them?"

"I believe we should," I affirmed, my voice steady and unwavering. "Let's approach this. We'll set it up so Detective Mercer listens to their confession in the other room. We can ensure we gather all the evidence we need."

I turned to the group, brows furrowing with deep consideration, and spoke with heartfelt conviction. "We ought to bring Dakota into this meeting," I proposed, my voice resonating. "He deserves to learn who's been siphoning from his organization. I hold details that will jolt him. It's only right he receives this revelation from us." My words conveyed a steadfast resolve, underscoring the significance of my suggestion.

I dialed Dakota first. There was a moment of hesitation before I pressed the call button. He answered. I detected the surprise in his voice as I explained the situation's urgency and asked him to come to my house. After a short pause, his curiosity got the better of him, and he agreed to come, his voice filled with intrigue.

Next, I called Jessica Numan, the alleged fraudster. I extended the invitation. I sensed the apprehension in her voice. There was a noticeable pause before she accepted, the uncertainty in her tone unmistakable.

An evident stress hung in the air. The pieces of this intricate puzzle were now set, and the stage was ready for a confrontation that would reshape the course of the organization Hope for Tomorrow. With their motivations and secrets, each participant was on a collision course with truth and consequences.

Dakota, the CEO of our organization, arrived, his attire exuding an air of authority in his well-fitted charcoal gray suit. Confidence and curiosity mingled in his attitude as he stepped through the doorway. His dark eyes swept the room, a blend of anticipation and intrigue dancing within them.

The women and Seth extended warm greetings, engaging in light conversation to alleviate the palpable anxiety. Compliments flowed for Dakota's attire, and a faint, appreciative smile tugged at the corners of his lips. We strived to cultivate an atmosphere of friendliness, ensuring Dakota was at ease in what promised to be a charged meeting.

After Dakota, Jessica Numan arrived. Her confident behavior was subdued, and she appeared aware of the situation.

I greeted Jessica with a warm smile. "Hi, Jessica. How are you?"

Rebeccah joined in, her tone was friendly. "I love your outfit, Jessica. You look great."

Jessica smiled, though her tension was intense. "Thanks."

"Please, have a seat," I said, gesturing to a nearby chair. "We're glad you're here."

Jessica sat down, and Rebeccah continued with light-hearted small talk. "So, how was your day?"

"It was okay," she replied, a bit more relaxed.

We all smiled as I began, "As you know, we investigated alleged fraud within Hope for Tomorrow. We have put together many details, and someone's been getting very rich at the expense of the children".

Holli continued, "Dakota, we found out a lot about you. You grew up in a modest neighborhood and come from a humble background. Your parents worked hard, your mom a registered nurse, and your father a plumber to provide for the family. In college, you were at the top of your class, which brought the best internship and job offers. You became greedy with a sense of entitlement. Over the years, you have grown accustomed to a lavish lifestyle and sought ways to maintain it without suspicion falling on you. You enjoy the attention of beautiful women. We had an exciting conversation with Sarai Bennett, the finance manager. You two were an item, weren't you?"

"Yes," Dakota stated. "Dating someone in your company is not a crime."

I chimed, "But it is cause for removal from your position as CEO, so it was kept quiet. She told us about the affair and showed us the non-profit's balance sheet.

Tampani commented, "But it doesn't mean I am stealing money!"

"You're right," I said, my voice measured. "We understood you didn't steal the money because you can't access the accounts. Let me explain further. I installed the financial system for Hope for Tomorrow with a dual-layer security feature when I discovered inconsistencies in the fiscal records. You and others can access the front-end interface, but a sophisticated back-end program runs in the background, accessible only to those with advanced system knowledge."

Seth interjected, "Yes, it's a separate encrypted interface allowing for more intricate transactions. Only a few high-level employees and board members had the expertise and clearance to operate it."

Holli added, "We suspect this back-end program is used to manipulate records and carry out fraudulent transactions. Only three people have access- Sarai, Samantha, and Bobby Guzman. You, Dakota, did not have access to or the technical know-how to operate this hidden system."

I began, my tone measured, "We received many tips implicating your involvement, and while they were convincing, we didn't allocate much time to investigate you. There were also anonymous tips left on my front doorstep, pointing fingers at Emily Raymond. I witnessed her in a heated argument with another board member, but we didn't delve into her case. I can affirm the individual behind those front door tips has been unmasked. It appears they attempted a double red herring, which proved ineffective."

Jessica's composure wavered as her glance fixed on the world outside the picture window framing my backyard.

"We only disclosed our investigation into Hope for Tomorrow to one person, a matter we'll address later," I continued.

Holli took the floor, "We exerted significant effort to uncover who possessed an uncanny knowledge of our every move. The pursuit led us to the unsettling revelation a mole infiltrated the board's ranks, feeding critical inside information to external sources. This fact confirmed during last night's gala. The mole in question is Bobby Guzman."

At this revelation, Jessica's face drained of color, and tiny beads of sweat began to form on her forehead. Her mannerisms underwent a stark transformation. She witnessed the confrontation with an air of confidence, almost relishing the prospect of her former employer's downfall. However, as it became evident that Dakota was not implicated, her once self-assured expression gave way to confusion and growing concern.

"It wasn't until we set a trap," Rebeccah began, her voice measured. "A trap offered convenient access and a fabricated document containing codes and numbers. Jessica, we had surveillance on you last night. We witnessed you and Bobby entering the hallway, engaging in covert activity, and pocketing the code sheet before departing. It's all captured on tape."

Jessica's eyes darted among us, searching for any signs of doubt or indications the evidence against Dakota still held weight. Her body language shifted, growing more guarded.

The sinking realization the blame might soon be placed upon her began to seep into Jessica's consciousness. She made a valiant effort to maintain a veneer of composure, but the undercurrents of anxiety in her eyes. Her customary assertiveness appeared to waver, and a visible discomfort settled upon her. Nervous fingers tapped the table's edge, a telltale sign of her growing unease. It was as though the gravity of her actions had caught up with her.

I took a deep breath and continued, "I realize you left those messages."

Breanna added her tone firm, "We were well aware of Jessica's involvement even before we bolstered security in the computer system. She had been using employees at Sparkling Clean Solutions to gather sensitive knowledge from the discarded office trash of Tampani's office. Combined with Bobby's insider knowledge, this ensured a steady flow of details and money."

Dakota interjected once more, his tone puzzled, "What does this have to do with me?"

"Nothing! We only wanted you to witness the thief stealing from the children," I asserted, my stare locked onto Dakota. Frustration and determination resonated in my voice.

Jessica broke her silence, trembling with regret and vulnerability, "It was never about the money. I just wanted to be recognized by a man who showed affection to every woman in the office but me."

Detective Mercer appeared from around the kitchen corner. Our plan worked, and he listened to the confession. A momentary silence fell over the room as he stood there, tall and composed, his face with a no-nonsense expression.

"I believe I've caught enough," he declared, his voice steady and commanding. "Come with me, Miss Numan; we must go to the station."

Jessica's eyes widened, and her face drained of color as she grasped the gravity of the situation. She resembled a deer caught in the blinding glare of headlights, paralyzed by the inevitability of her predicament. The burden of guilt pressed upon her, and the futility of evading the consequences loomed. Mercer's approach to Jessica was composed, ensuring she remained under control. His wealth of experience and unshakable confidence projected an aura of authority, leaving no doubt he held dominion over the unfolding events.

Holli took a step forward, extending a folder brimming with incriminating evidence. "We've compiled substantial proof linking Jessica Numan to the fraudulent activities at Hope for Tomorrow and Bobby Guzman as an accessory," she announced with resolve.

"Thank you," he replied, his voice tinged with professional gratitude. He maintained a composed exterior. A subtle flutter in his chest betrayed the moment's intensity. "Your diligence here has been exceptional. This evidence will prove invaluable in constructing a strong case against Numan."

Holli nodded, a small, self-assured smile gracing her lips. "We trust the evidence will tell the story."

Mercer recited Jessica's Miranda rights, maintaining a firm and respectful demeanor. He led her towards a waiting police car. Jessica's countenance shifted from defiance to a mixture of regret and resignation as the car drove away, leaving her to face the consequences of her choices.

Dakota, attempting to excuse himself, found his path blocked by my firm look and the presence of another folder. I began, my voice tinged with resolve, "You understand I'll have to take all these particulars to the board. It will likely make headlines in the newspapers. I would advise you to consult your attorney and find a way to resign. It won't harm Hope for Tomorrow or its benefactors."

He met my stare, his eyes heavy with guilt.

I continued, "There's one more matter you should discuss with your attorney – child support."

His expression shifted to one of confusion by my revelation.

I pressed on, holding up a paternity test conducted over three years ago. "This test shows you are the father of Makenzie's child."

Without a word, he excused himself and went to his car. His future became shrouded in doubt. I understood justice would follow its course, but for now, my focus shifted to the impending Board meeting. It was time to unveil the secret, ensuring Hope for Tomorrow could move forward with the integrity and transparency it deserved.

Chapter 10

I stood there, watching the police car disappear around the corner with Jessica Numan in the back seat.

Holli exhaled, her posture relaxing as the tension released. "That's a weight off our shoulders. Jessica is facing the consequences she deserves."

Rebeccah nodded, her eyes never leaving the spot where the police car vanished. "The children at Hope for Tomorrow can breathe a little easier now."

Breanna's contemplative tone revealed her thoughtful side. "It's astonishing to think about how far we've come. It's been a rollercoaster of emotions from uncovering the fraud to confronting the culprits."

The day unfolded, we took a break to enjoy a light lunch. I seized the moment to brew another pot of coffee, ensuring our collective energy remained high. Holli, with her meticulous attention to detail, reviewed our evidence. Rebeccah, the voice of reason, scrutinized our arguments, ensuring they were sound and compelling. Breanna kept our spirits elevated, infusing us with the determination to move forward.

In the late afternoon, I retreated to my home office to finalize my presentation for the gathering. Every piece of evidence was organized, awaiting their moment to be revealed to the board.

We drove to Hope for Tomorrow's offices, focused on the board meeting. The room was a hive of activity, buzzing with the focused energy of our team as we readied ourselves for the pivotal moment ahead.

The documents strewn across the table were visual evidence of the months of dedication and hard work we poured into this investigation. I stood before my fellow directors. I took a deep breath and spoke. "I'm thrilled to report that the gala was a tremendous success," I said with a smile. "Thanks to the unwavering support of our generous donors, sponsors, and attendees, we raised $150,000 for Hope for Tomorrow."

The members gasped in surprise and delight. The donation would impact the organization's programs and initiatives. I continued, "With this amount, we can now take critical steps towards expanding our reach and enhancing our services for the children in need. We can invest in educational programs, healthcare facilities, and support systems that will provide a brighter future for the kids we serve."

My smile faded as I shifted the conversation to the fraud investigation. It contrasted the previous jubilant atmosphere, but it was a reality we couldn't ignore.

"We must address Bobby Guzman's involvement in the fraudulent activities," I said.

"That's a serious accusation. What evidence do you have?" Erin asked.

"We have substantial evidence linking them to the financial discrepancies," I said.

Emily inquired, "And what about Tampani's actions?"

"Dating subordinates is a violation. We must address this issue delicately." I commented.

Another board member asked, "How do we proceed from here?"

I suggested, "We need to conduct a thorough investigation and take appropriate action based on the results."

It was an uncomfortable truth, but we understood we couldn't ignore the wrongdoing. My fellow members' expressions transformed from disbelief to steely resolve. Nods of understanding and agreement rippled through the room, mirroring the gravity of the situation. The sight of furrowed brows and the occasional clenched fists indicated the depth of emotions stirred within us.

The Chairman of the board, a figure of authority at the charity, somberly stepped to the front of the room. He held a letter in his hands, and his expression conveyed the gravity of its contents. "I have received a resignation letter from Dakota Tampani, our CEO." His words reverberated through the room, and a peaceful silence fell over everyone. It was a moment of profound significance, marking a pivotal turn in the organization's history.

The Chairman continued, "I have shared this letter with each of you, and it is now time to discuss its acceptance." He paused, allowing the implications of Dakota Tampani's resignation to sink in.

There was a secret ballot vote, and the board members reached a unanimous decision.

The chairman announced, with a collective nod of agreement, "The board has accepted his resignation."

Epilogue

The following day raced by like a whirlwind of activity, each passing moment carrying the electric energy of impending change. Our group gathered at my favorite rooftop restaurant, which became a sanctuary for celebrations and reflections. We ascended to the restaurant's elevated terrace. The anticipation of the evening ahead hung in the air, a palpable undercurrent beneath our shared excitement.

The sights that greeted us atop the terrace were nothing short of breathtaking. In its golden descent, the sun painted the sky with orange and pink hues, casting a warm, ethereal glow over the cityscape. The restaurant's elegant decor, adorned with flickering candles and delicate fairy lights, created an enchanting ambiance, inviting us to revel in the moment's magic.

The sounds of our gathering were a harmonious blend of laughter, animated chatter, and the clinking of glasses. Conversations flowed. The attentive and welcoming restaurant staff added their melodic notes to the symphony of voices, ensuring our celebration unfolded seamlessly.

I scanned the familiar faces, noting with a hint of disappointment everyone was present except for Holli. The atmosphere shifted with a delightful surprise before we could ponder her absence for too long. Moments later, a new pair graced our gathering as if on cue, and my eyes widened in pleasant astonishment.

Holli was walking through the restaurant's entrance, her radiant smile lighting up the room. What caught our attention was the sight of her arm-in-arm with John Mercer, the man who had been instrumental in unraveling the mysteries we encountered.

The group's reaction was a chorus of surprised laughter and playful teasing. I greeted them with exclamations, "Well, isn't this a surprise!" and "You two make quite the entrance!"

The restaurant's ambiance shifted to accommodate the unexpected addition, embracing their presence with open arms.

"No, you should not be shocked!" Holli chimed in with a playful smile on her face. "I'll spend a few extra days in your lovely town."

There was laughter and joy all around the table. It turned out Holli and Detective Mercer had been keeping a secret from the rest of us. We all smiled as we raised our glasses to celebrate their newfound happiness.

"Cheers to love and surprises!" Breanna toasted, raising her glass, and we all joined in.

I sat on the rooftop terrace, surrounded by joyful chatter and the clinking of glasses. I couldn't help but drift to the uncertain path ahead for Bobby Guzman and Jessica Numan within the legal system. This reflection bore the weight of their actions' intended and unintended consequences.

The possibility of Bobby and Jessica facing the justice system was now a stark reality, casting a shadow over the night's festivities. I wondered how their lives, once intertwined with Hope for Tomorrow, would unfold in the harsh light of legal scrutiny.

"Does anyone understand what the future holds for Jessica and Bobby?" I inquired.

John's tone was contemplative, "If they choose to cooperate, the judge might consider leniency. It's in their hands, and their willingness to cooperate could influence the outcome."

Breanna posed a question that weighed on all our minds, "But do you think this will impact Hope for Tomorrow?"

I replied, "Hope for Tomorrow is a remarkable organization serving countless people in Clarkston. The actions of a few should not overshadow the good it does."

Holli reached for her glass, "I hope Dakota takes care of Makenzie and provides the support she deserves. She has faced challenges and adversity, but with proper child support, her daughter can have the opportunities she deserves for a bright future."

The drinks passed, and Seth cleared his throat and announced he had something important to share. The excitement in the room heightened, and all eyes were on him and me. "It may be a while until the ladies are together to catch more bad guys. Samantha and I do have an announcement. Something we have meant to tell you ever since you all arrived in Clarkston." Seth began, his smile matching the twinkle in his eyes as he held me close.

I thought about the secret of where I worked and what I did for a living, but I had a better secret to tell. I blushed, experiencing the warmth of everyone's attention. With a deep breath, I shared the most beautiful news of all, "I'm pregnant."

Acknowledgements

Creating a book transcends the solitary act of typing on an author's keyboard. It's a collaborative effort involving numerous individuals, each contributing to the tapestry that brings forth the mesmerizing worlds an author unveils. This book stands as a testament to that collective endeavor. Behind its pages lies a dedicated and talented team I would like to thank- Tiffany Vega, Sara Davil & Lia Thomas, for fervently weaving together a narrative brimming with strength, transformation, and the enduring bonds of friendship. A heartfelt appreciation extends to my cover artist, Sadia Asif. Your creative vision has given this tale its visual essence, breathing life onto its cover and beyond. Yet, paramount among my acknowledgments is to my beloved family. To my wife, Holli, and daughters, Breanna, Rebeccah, and Samantha—you are the heartbeat of my inspiration. Your unwavering love and encouragement have been the guiding light throughout this journey. I cherish you all deeply.

Crafting the stories within the Investigation Series has been a labor of love, dear readers. While this series may have concluded, the tales of

Holli, Breanna, Rebeccah, and Samantha are far from over. Though they may not share the same book's pages again, each character is set to embark on their individual journey within a separate series, all slated for a grand debut in 2025.

Stay tuned with keen anticipation as HojoPress Publishing unveils a wealth of new books, each laden with narratives poised to gently pull at your heartstrings. Look forward to their arrival in late fall of 2024.

Become a part of our vibrant reader community by visiting us at www.hojopresspublishing.com, and connect with us on LinkedIn, Facebook, and Instagram. Our regular updates inform us about our latest projects, exclusive discounts, and early release dates for special community products.

John Russell